A Way Back Home

a novel based on actual events

S.L. Kowalski

Published by Mark J. Pugliese

2012

A Way Back Home

Copyright © 2012 by S.L. Kowalski

All rights reserved. This book or any portion thereof
may not be reproduced or used in any manner whatsoever
without the express written permission of the publisher
except for the use of brief quotations in a book review.

Published by Mark J. Pugliese | Utica, MI

Edited by Jenny Bones

Cover art by Jeffery Thompson
Cover design and page layout by S.L. Kowalski

First Edition

ISBN 978-0615754680

slkowalski.com

Explicit Content Warning

A Way Back Home is the harrowing tale of a boy's journey through the depths of incest and violence. It is a story based on actual events, told from the author's best recollections through long-repressed memories of intense pain and heartache.

The book is a traumatic read and not recommended for anyone who is easily triggered or offended. Mr. Kowalski recounts these dark few months of his late adolescence with unapologetic candor. The unsuspecting reader is swept into the warped reality of these events and carried along the downward spiral of physical, emotional and sexual abuse.

> *When 57-year old Jane finds herself abandoned by her husband, she turns to her son for the companionship she so desperately craves. No one would suspect the twisted and unnatural events unfolding behind the closed curtains of her middle-class, middle-American home. No one would come to rescue her prey.*

> *Even as young Jack tries to fend off his seductive, manipulative and emotionally-starved mother, he finds his body betraying him time and time again. Trying to make sense of the senseless, Jack's physical and emotional health begin to unravel as violence and lust hijack his world.*

At a time when a teenage boy is just beginning to define his sexuality, few events could cause more damage.

This is a story that must be told and a subject that demands exposure.

"Brilliant and vile and terrifying. It's how 'The Catcher in the Rye' should have been written."
                                                    ~ *Jackie Trippier Holt*

With love and affection,
for this book and more,
for especially this book and more,
I dedicate the words inside to Jenny Bones, my love, my life.

You save me and release me every day.
You give space when no space is due.
For you especially my heart and more,
with love and affection.

Thank you

With humble regard for everyone that passes through my life,
with regret at the distance I create,
I offer words on top of words on top of my heart where I find all of
you inside.

In order of appearance, known and unknown alike:

Stephen G. Colyer, for turning me on to reading in the first place.
Roger Zelazny, late, great style from which I sift.
Lawrence Pike, late, cantankerous poet who showed me the fire.
Art Ritas, with you I found in words my voice and reason.
Kris D'Arcy, with you I found in words my heart and soul.
Derek Von Ecker, for reminding me about youth, fire and passion.
Dr. Trish Pich, for scrambling my brains into action.

A special thanks to,
Jackie Trippier Holt, for your support, guidance and friendship.

Contents

Chapter 1

"Just go home, Jack. I don't have anything for you."

Fifty degrees outside, when winter and spring collide, the balance point of heating, air conditioning and nature. I, myself, felt off balance. I emerged from behind the dumpster and tossed the broom and dustpan over by the shop's back door. No one else was around, but that wouldn't have stopped me. "I suppose there's no work tomorrow either."

"Jack, tomorrow's Saturday," my Dad said, quietly exasperated, wincing at the implied failure in my words. He pinched off his cigarette butt and flicked it into the dumpster. "Just come in after school on Monday and I'll find something."

Whatever. Asshole.

The edge of anger always sifted our words. Anger, fear, frustration, both of us trapped in the same skin. Our arguments needed no context. Insanity needed no context. The world had done us wrong: Our shared mantra. The gas utility decimated his business. Cancer decimated his wife. Drugs and stupid friends decimated his youngest son.

He turned away, suddenly sad, and disappeared through the door. I picked up the broom and dustpan and followed him into the shop, but he'd already disappeared up to the front office.

His heating business floundered on the edge of the city. I remembered how great it was to go to work with him in the summer when I was twelve. Anything to get away from the house.

I sat in my car and felt sorry for myself. I dug in the ashtray for my last joint and felt lost. Not lost, blurry. Everything was blurry. No lines existed between employer and employee, between father and son. Failing grades and beautifully fucked up friends somehow stood both in front of me and decades away.

I wasted the hour drive home and missed the transition from urban to rural, the slow blend from gray concrete to green trees, the smell of exhaust, machines and restaurant grease to wildflowers, fresh water and the farmer's raw, fresh earth. I drove and raced toward the future, a dog chasing its tail. Like my father before me chasing an imaginary point in time, I refused to acknowledge the beautiful instant of my life.

Chasing, running, searching finding, dismissing; at seventeen I was already exhausted.

Although, it was Friday night, I thought, climbing out of my car and feeling the long drive and mild high rush through my legs. More drugs and some booze: The only prescription I knew for a perfect life. I cut through the garage and opened the door leading directly to the dining room, anticipating a shower and more fun with the future.

Except. Mom crying.

She sat at the dining room table, still in her robe wrapped around herself, and looked up at me with hysteria on her features. She crushed a cigarette butt into an overflowing ashtray and attempted to push her gray-red hair into some sort of order.

"Jack...", She said as if surprised at my arrival, or the time of day, or who knew what. "Oh, Jack...."

My first thought – the instant of my first thought – was I didn't want to waste a moment of my precious future on her. She looked like she hadn't moved from her chair since the morning. Still in her robe, barefoot, curled and crunched within herself.

Had the cancer returned, I wondered.

"Jack, he's left us," she mumbled, reaching for her exhausted pack of cigarettes.

"Left us? Who's left us?" I quickly gathered a few thoughts, but she was already standing, dropping the cigarette pack and squeezing herself. "He's left us," she said again, second-guessing herself from rolling the same thought around for hours. "Did you see him today?" she asked, taking a few tentative steps toward me.

I backed against the wall, searching the wilderness of her features.

"See who?" I asked. "Mom, what –"

"He's gone," she said sternly, loosening up and staring at me like I should understand completely. "Your father is gone."

"Gone?"

"Yes. Did you see him?"

"Yes... what? What are you –"

"Of course you did," she answered herself, shaking with a bit of nervous fear and anger. "He's left us, Jack. Did he happen to mention that?"

I stared at her as she stepped closer. I just saw him an hour ago, I thought. What did she mean? What did she mean he's left us?

She stood in front of me, she stood too close to me, I couldn't decide. I felt her hair on my chin and I couldn't decide. Her anxious energy, I thought. Something about her nervous energy. What did she mean he's left us?

"Your father moved out today, Jack," she said quietly, reaching up and touching my cheek. She released me and hugged herself again, for an instant. Then, "He's not coming home."

"Mom," I said, finding my voice again. "What are you talking about? I just saw him –"

"Who is she, Jack?" Mom asked, pushing her dirty green eyes into me. "*Who is she?*"

"Who –"

"It doesn't matter, does it?" She dismissed herself and pushed her hand up my chest. "Of course not. Why would it matter? He's gone."

Again she released me and stood so close to me, staring up at me, searching, staring, studying something in me. I couldn't let go of her eyes: jagged yellow edges surrounding deep sea green.

"You won't leave me, will you, Jack? Tell me you won't leave me."

Her pupils undulated in a slow rhythm, growing, shrinking, growing.

"Tell me!" she growled under her breath, catching herself too late, brushing my face then chest with her fingertips. She forced an awkward smile and waited.

I said nothing, watching the twist in her eyes as she rubbed my chest harder. "Tell me, Jackie," she whispered, stepping up on her toes, then back down, now pushing both hands against my chest. "Please, honey, tell me you won't leave me."

Her eyes deepened, darkening into a hard, burnt green. She pushed her hands slowly and roughly up my chest, back to my waist, searching my eyes with such a strange intent I began to panic. Mom was a tiny woman, not even five feet tall. I could have easily pushed her away.

I should have picked her up and thrown her across the room.

Instead I stood perfectly still, paralyzed by something in her, or something digging so deeply in me I had to force myself to breath.

"Don't leave me, Jackie," she whispered again. Her hands slid to my belt. "Tell me you won't ever leave me."

I said nothing as she roughly loosened my belt, flipped my pants button open and yanked my zipper down.

"I love you so much, Jackie," she hissed, never taking her eyes off me as she shoved her hand down my pants and took a firm hold of my stiff cock. "You love me, too, Jackie. I know you do." She squirmed once and smiled, working her hand down to my balls and squeezing. "I love you so much, honey...."

My head swirled. Every blood vessel swelled ready to explode. I couldn't take my eyes off her. I pressed my back against the wall and agonized over the soreness of her touch.

Her eyes lightened, drifted, almost caught fire right in front of me. Something, I thought. Something inside burned along with her eyes. I felt nothing and I felt everything as she yanked my pants and underwear passed my hips. She carved a wild grin across her face and rapidly pumped my cock.

I had to scream. I had to push her away. I had to pick her up and throw her across the room. I did nothing except follow her eyes down as she knelt in front of me and took me into her mouth for a moment.

Cold sweat immediately soaked my clothes.

She kissed my cock, licking and slurping around it, never taking her eyes off me. "Don't ever leave me, Jackie," she said quietly as she took me in her mouth and sucked.

She forced my cock down her throat and held it, letting her eyes glaze over into mine. She refused to let up until she gagged, then kissing, pumping, licking, sucking over and over again.

"See how much I love you, my Jackie? See how much I love you...?"

Something, she said. She said something. I stood mesmerized by her, enthralled by her and by something in me, something inside me, waking up – realizing something buried inside me.

I fell into her eyes, pouring myself into her, flooding into her.

Her flaming green eyes watered over. Mascara and tears ran down her face. She attacked my cock in a crazed frenzy.

My mind ripped open and I grabbed the back of her head and thrust into her several times. Her body shook in my grip. She moaned, gurgled and collapsed in my hands as I drained myself into her.

I released her and pushed her back, finally breaking eye contact. She fell back on her ass, gasping, drawing breath and shaking. She hunched forward and wrapped her arms around herself.

Mom looked small and helpless. She shivered and kept her head down. I caught my breath quickly and stood apart from the wall. I stared down at her, watching her, studying her, failing to understand anything inside me.

I reached out and touched her head. She flinched and wouldn't look up. "Please don't hate me, Jackie," she said with tears in her voice. "I love you so much. Please don't hate me."

She resisted my lifting her face up to mine. "Please don't hate me...."

"I don't hate you...." I couldn't say the word *Mom*. I couldn't name her anything. Not Jane, her name. Not anything.

"I love you, Jackie," she said again, still refusing to look at me.

"I know," I replied, running my hand under her chin and gently lifting up.

Then, suddenly as if all life depended on it, she blurted, "Please don't leave me," and sank back to the floor.

"I won't," I said, feeling the truth in my words. "I won't leave you."

Mom looked up at me and cast a wet, embarrassed smile. Something soft inside her struggled for a moment when she saw my limp cock hanging in front of her. Something soft for an instant, then she yanked my pants up and pushed herself off the floor.

"You must be starving," she said, freakishly becoming my mother. She smoothed her robe and pushed her messy wet hair aside. "I look a mess," she said, looking down at herself and again offering an embarrassed smile. "I haven't even dressed today."

I opened my mouth and again couldn't name her anything. My stomach ached inside as if suddenly filled with acid. I had no interest in food, but again she told me I was starved.

"I'm sorry, Jackie," she said. "I will always have dinner for you, honey." She turned away before I could reply, as if I could reply, and walked into the kitchen. "I'll have everything you want waiting for you."

Yes, I thought, suddenly craving a shower. Everything I want.

I had no idea what, exactly, I wanted. But I knew somehow she'd let me know soon enough.

Chapter 2

Fear.

I stood in the shower as long as possible, barely feeling the water pour over me. Through the haze I smelled her cooking something, warming up something. I couldn't define it then, the fear. I couldn't name the feeling any more than I could name the woman on the other side of the wall who sucked my cock and cooked me dinner.

Yet, something in the moment remained eerily normal, completely acceptable on some interior, inaccessible level of my thoughts. Despite the discomfort and confusion, I relaxed in the fear without realization. I forced myself to fit inside my uneven skin.

What choice did I have? I asked myself – or told myself, or barely sensed the words. Somewhere out there my father had broken free. He would not turn me away.

Except he'd left me here, hadn't he? Alone, with her. He'd left me alone with her, defenseless – *he knew about her fiery green eyes* – and he ran.

Friends, then, I thought. I could crash on the couch at a few places, at least until I figured a few things out. Dave, Eddie, their parents were cool. I had known them both for years.

But something else bothered me. I turned off the shower and simply stood, shivering as the water evaporated on my skin.

I am in the middle of my life, I thought, or heard inside, not understanding what it meant.

"Dinner," she said through the door.

I froze and lost my thought. Her close, low toned voice crawled up my spine.

"I made you some dinner, Jackie."

I stared through the wavy shower door toward the bathroom door. I hadn't locked the door against her. Then, "Okay," I said, listening to myself talk. I felt her standing on the other side, felt her heart pounding, felt the nervous energy boiling inside her.

I waited her out, naked and cold behind the shower door, unable to make a sound, to slide the door open or expose myself to her despite the closed bathroom door.

What was I supposed to do?

What was I supposed to say?

My cock stiffened and I couldn't stop shaking.

I slid the door open and dried quickly, deciding to leave, to go somewhere, anywhere. I thought about Dad but didn't know where he lived or how to get a hold of him. I couldn't believe he left and didn't say shit to me. "*Just come in after school on Monday and I'll find something....*"

How about, *Oh, bytheway I movedthefuckout?*

Yeah....

I dropped the towel on the floor and reached for my underwear.

"I've got dinner, honey," she said, her voice right next to me, cutting through the door between us. "Did you hear me, Jackie?"

"Yes," I replied, standing immediately up and freezing in place. I stared at the doorknob, seeing it unlocked, waiting for it to open. My hard on ached and I squeezed tears out of my eyes. "Yes," I said again, unable to shake the nervous tone out of my voice.

She moved away. I felt her move away. I sensed her so strongly, so deeply, as if I watched her every movement, as if I lived inside her skin. I blinked and looked around and hated the bathroom. I hated the confinement. I dressed quickly, never keeping my eyes from the doorknob. I combed my wet hair and refused to look at my eyes in the mirror.

I opened the door, found the hallway empty, and smelled spaghetti sauce. What was I supposed to do, I wondered. What was I supposed to say?

I stepped around the corner, looked through the kitchen and into the dining room. She stood next to the table, still barefoot but now in a very short bath robe. She stood so still, so erect. I felt nervous energy pour out of her and collide with my own confusion. She'd put makeup on and combed her auburn hair into a pony tail.

"Jack..." she said quietly, stepping back as I came around the kitchen counter. She'd set two plates, mine in my dad's place.

"I'm not very –"I began; then stopped at her eyes.

Soft. So soft and frightened, pale green, lost in distance and pain. "Please, Jackie," she said so quietly. "It's yours now. Please let me sit next to you."

So, I did.

I did and we both picked at our food. The room was wrong, of course, the angle, the objects, the view out the dining room window. This was not my seat, not at this table.

She put her fork down and folded her hands in her lap. Her robe opened enough for me to see she wore nothing underneath. Her tits swelled and released with each breath.

No, I thought.

I watched her not so subtle squirm and squiggle. She tucked her short legs under the chair and let the robe open to her pussy.

Just, no, goddamnit bitch.

What was she doing? Wasn't she just going to let it rest, let it pass, let it remain one awkward incident?

"Are you going out tonight?" she asked so softly I had to lean to hear her. Before I could think, let alone answer, she continued, "Maybe you could stay home tonight." She looked up suddenly and I was surprised by the gentleness of her eyes. I expected fire and found only fear and awkwardness.

I understood something inside her then: another nameless thing, I could barely imagine.

"We could watch TV," she was saying. "I know it's not –"

"I'll stay," I said without realizing my words. My cock stiffened and I dropped angry eyes to her tits, to her bare legs. I caught myself and looked up, finding another version of nervous innocence in her. Again something similar inside, again no effort to cover herself; I saw only fear staring back.

My fear, her fear, without realizing my thoughts I smiled.

She smiled back without fire, without panic. She sat surrendered, exposed, open, honest. Fear filled the space around us and she reveled in it, lived it, breathed it, washed her body and mind with it.

She sat back for an instant, exposing a thin stripe of bare flesh and allowing me a glimpse of red-gray bush and stretch marks on her belly. She gathered our plates without a word.

I watched the sun set outside across the farmer's field. Our house, her house, Dad's house, whoever the hell's house it was sat on a hill in the middle of nowhere. There were neighbors around, a dozen or so scattered on five-acre plots, but I never felt so alone.

I could leave, of course. I could get up and leave, as I would have, as I should have. Go out, find Dave and Eddie, get as high as I could and come home as late as possible, if at all.

I could do that, but instead I sat and watched the burned up sky rest heavy on the evening.

She wiped the table, letting her tits shake for me, letting me see her bare legs, her strong thighs, her long, painted fingernails and the clear path inside her. Sad, distant, pale green submission radiated out of her.

Surrender covered her – and I sat overwhelmed by her, enveloped by her, at least in this moment, this everlasting instant. Again, a deep connection, a familiar vacuum – fuck I didn't understand any of the shit going on inside me.

But I couldn't leave her like that, not like that – and I knew I would sit and watch television with her, let her expose herself to me, let her satisfy *the something* inside her. In the morning we would talk, I decided. Or not. We would talk, or not, and this thing would be behind us.

I walked into the family room, turned on the news and heard none of it. I sat on the couch and watched her flit about between the kitchen and the dining room. Waves of nervous energy flowed between us, twisting me into knots. I looked away and watched television, finding the latest murder, scandal, state of the economy and weather equally unimportant.

She came in with an ashtray and a cup of coffee. "Here, Jack," she said, setting them by Dad's recliner. "Sit here and have coffee."

I looked up at her as she set the items down and smiled awkwardly at me. "Please, Jackie...."

I couldn't call her "Mom" and I couldn't call her Jane. I couldn't call her bitch or whore, either, so I sat and looked from her to the coffee to the recliner, and back to her. She adjusted the robe loosely, taking time to fix it just so, to reveal everything, display everything, offer everything.

Her tits, her nipples, her pussy, all in perfect view against the orange evening light. But still her eyes shone pale green, like an ocean at rest. She smiled like someone's mother and left the room for her own coffee.

Words all but exploded out of me, but I said nothing and absorbed the internal impact of... what? What was she doing? What the hell was she doing? Tits, ass and the happy mother? Upset at Dad? Yes, of course, Dad leaving, his place at the table, his recliner. Nerves, yes, hers, mine and ours, and what the hell was going on with her – and me?

"Thank you, Jack," she said, entering the room and setting her coffee and ashtray by the couch. She curled up, exposed her pussy and sat back into the couch, wrapping everything and nothing around herself.

Her fear vanished, replaced by an absence or something, a hole, I didn't know, or didn't want to know. A void, a vacuum, too much space, or no space at all – but that *was it*, then, wasn't it? She found her comfort, her space, in a crazy place where you suck your own son's cock.

So fuck it, early evening with plenty of light remaining, I sat in my father's chair and drank his coffee with my mother's pussy in full view.

She pretended to watch TV and absently smoothed her robe, touching herself, brushing herself, pouring herself at me. She turned quickly, caught me looking at her, smiled, sipped, smoked and turned back to the news.

She gave me everything I wanted that night, of course. She refilled my coffee, fetched snacks later on and filled the night with light comments on whatever show we watched.

I sat and drifted from near panic attacks to absolute certainty she was on the verge of a nervous breakdown. I told myself – desperately told myself – she would be fine tomorrow. She probably wouldn't remember any of this, and I needed to let her be, let her ride out the shock of Dad's leaving in whatever way she could.

I burned it into my brain like a mantra until she decided it was time for bed. We listened to the late news, listened to new versions of the same stories and at the end she announced it was her bedtime.

"Thank you, honey," she said, rising off the couch and taking the two steps toward me. "I know you didn't want to stay here on a Friday night."

She bent down and cupped my face before I could react. She kissed my cheek and gave me a full shot of her tits. She didn't let go, paused for effect and kissed me again.

So controlled, I thought. No fire, no submission, so tight I couldn't read her at all. She kissed my lips quickly, something we had never done, and stood back up. "I'll see you in the morning," she said simply and disappeared.

I sat in the recliner for a moment and realized my cock was so hard it hurt. What was she doing? Okay, then, okay. Her husband left her and she was afraid, confused, terrified, okay. Okay then.

Her sexuality tore through my mind and I suddenly hated her. I hated her quickly and just as quickly pushed it aside. She was sad and afraid, I told myself. I pushed myself out of the chair and stared into the darkest part of the house.

Her bedroom light came on in that instant, colors revealed where I craved only shades of gray. I walked through the dining room and kitchen and stood at her opened door. She dropped the robe and turned at my arrival.

Naked, calm without sense of invitation; without turning away, she offered a hesitant smile and made no effort to cover herself.

I stepped into the room and she shrank back.

Bitch, I thought, moving around the bed and resisting the urge to slap her. What did she think? What did she think she was doing to me?

Bitch.

"Jack..." she said, as if she hadn't expected this, asked for it; designed, created and executed it in her own twisted mind.

I said nothing and started taking off my clothes. I was going to fuck her, I thought, using someone else's mind, or maybe it was my own mind. Either way, I knew I was going to fuck the shit out of her.

"What are you doing?" she asked, then backed away a step, realizing her own nakedness. "Jack, I...", she tried again, only to retake the step toward me and cast her eyes to the bed between us.

Unbelievable.

I stood naked in front of her with a hard on aimed directly at her. Cold fear and sweat covered me inside and out. I felt foolish and ashamed. What was I doing?

Then, "Get in bed," I said with someone else's voice.

She stood still for a moment, so relaxed, so calm, and she studied me, stared at me, almost laughed at me as a mother to a foolish, awkward child.

No, I thought. She wouldn't turn this around on me. This was not on me.

Her expression didn't change. She never questioned anything, struggled with anything, sought a new tact, or a different approach. Words and actions collided inside her, as if nothing deep inside... or something – I thought, losing momentum.

"Jack," she whispered across the bed. "Please don't do this."

I didn't say anything because I didn't know what to say.

She pulled the bed sheets back and slid into bed. "Turn off the light," she said with someone else's voice. "Please."

I complied and climbed into bed next to her. What was I doing? Why was I doing this? I had to leave her alone. She had to get around everything. She just spent the day crying because her husband left her. Of course she was confused, angry and hurt.

What was I doing?

She spread her legs next to me and drew my attention. "You have to use this," she said matter-of-factly, showing me a tube of something.

She pushed the sheets down and I watched her rub her pussy, working the lubricant inside. She took my hand and put it on hers, showing me how to work her open. She lay back and stared up at the ceiling as I worked my fingers into my mother's pussy.

No, that wasn't her name or who she was anymore, I thought, opening her, breathing in her scent as well as my own.

She rolled toward me and immediately rubbed her clit on my thigh. Her hand found my cock before I smelled her hair and tasted her flesh.

Her absent, vacant, distraught eyes locked me in place. She stroked me hard, grabbed my balls and squeezed and pulled me over on top of her.

I slid right into her. She arched her back at my entrance and swallowed me whole. The wrinkles along her face and neck stretched as I slowly fucked her. I felt her thighs wrap around me and her pussy expand and contract around my cock.

She caught my eyes and smiled, suddenly driving her hips against me and quickening our pace. She smiled again and her face twisted into someone I'd never seen before. The color, tone and pitch of her eyes eluded me in the moonlight and she slid her hands down my back and rubbed my ass and thrust her hips wildly up at me.

I fucked her harder just to keep up with her, just to keep from being bucked off of her. A soft moan escaped her. "It's so good, my Jackie," she half whispered, half purred. Then, barely audible, "I'm so sorry, my Jackie."

Bitch.

I thrust harder and she grunted. I braced myself and thrust harder still. Her mouth opened and she drew a deep breath as if she'd been drowning or unable to breath. I pinched tears out of my eyes and saw what I was doing. I couldn't stop fucking her. I couldn't stop fucking my mother – and I panicked for a moment when I realized I couldn't stop.

I couldn't stop fucking her. Harder, I thrust into her, grabbing her shoulders and yanking her down into my manic thrusts. She dug her fingernails into me and hissed. I slammed my body down on hers. She dug her heels into me and hissed like an animal. Her hands clenched my skull and she pulled me all the way into her.

God, I thought. Ohmyfuckinggod. My eyes watered as I fucked her harder, dug in deeper and bore my full weight into each thrust.

Again, panic washed over me and I studied every feature, trying to recognize something familiar about her, anything to make me stop, to pull out of her, to throw myself through the window.

What was I doing?

What the fuck was I doing?

But she moaned and smiled and fucked like an animal. She focused on my eyes and snarled wildly at me – then, calm, in that instant, a soft smile and she tried to reach up and kiss me –

I pulled my face back and fucked her harder, slamming the head board against the wall and driving myself into her until she fell back, stretched her neck out and screamed.

Her body shook, tensed, released and exploded around me. She cried out and collapsed under me. My orgasm came as an afterthought as I watched her head roll to the side and her body go limp beneath me.

I stared at the side of her face and let my cock go limp inside of her.

She refused to look at me, to turn her head. I pulled out, rolled over and felt tears in my eyes.

I held my breath and panicked. I had fucked her. I fucked my own mother and had an orgasm inside her.

"It's okay, Jackie," I heard her say. She was next to me, touching me, rubbing my shoulder. "It's okay," she said again. She pulled me over and forced me to look at her.

Sympathy. Quiet calm. I was crying then, I realized, quietly crying the whole time. She touched my face so gently and kissed me on the lips.

I couldn't kiss her back, the tears, something, anyway, I couldn't kiss her back.

"No, my Jackie," she said so fucking sweetly. "Everything is alright." She laid her head on my chest and rubbed my legs.

How? How the hell was everything alright?

I rubbed her shoulders, then, and somewhere between horror and lust fell asleep with the scent of my mother upon me.

Chapter 3

I woke up to her sucking my cock.

No.

I woke up to her feeding on me like a vampire. She attacked and devoured me like a madwoman, a thing, a beast, an animal possessed. Strings of her warm, thick saliva bound the two of us together. She licked at me, furiously pumped my cock and cast a devious grin.

The fire returned.

I jerked and sat up, pressing my back against the head board. Morning light poured through the window, blinding me for an instant. I couldn't understand what was happening, where I was, who I was, who she was, why, how and nothing, all in an instant.

She stroked my cock wildly, never taking her flaring eyes off me. She leaned down and kept us locked together while she stole noisy mouthfuls of me. Her wretched smile hung like a demon between us.

She had no words, I knew somehow. Speech was not a part of this incarnation. Her moist lips dripped saliva and she couldn't take her hand off my cock. I knew she couldn't let go of it. Everything in the air felt like a wild animal guarding her survival.

She went back to sucking and slurping when she decided I wasn't going to take her meal away.

I grabbed a tight handful of hair and yanked her off my cock. She hissed and snarled and struggled in my grip. Her hand tightened around my cock and threatened a painful explosion.

"Please," she moaned in a deep, gurgling voice. "Please, Jackie, I love you so much." She spat the tangled words out of her throat. "You're so good to me."

What the hell was she talking about?

She pulled against my grip in her hair until I thought she would scalp herself. I let go and she lunged full force at my cock. She moaned and forced my cock down her throat, gagging herself and spitting up on me.

Tight pain rippled across my body and I tried to yank her off me again.

"I can take it, honey," she babbled and spit up again. "I can take all of you."

My cock ached from her painful attack and I didn't doubt her words.

But, what the freaking hell?

I remembered last night, the afternoon, dinner, the shower, the television, her pussy. None of it seemed real. None of it could be happening, I told myself.

I had to get out of there.

I had to get the hell out of there.

I grabbed her skull with two hands and threw her off me. She landed at the edge of the bed and scrambled toward my cock, darting her tongue out and pushing her matted hair out of her face.

"Get the hell away from me," I blurted, pushing her away.

She gasped and again pushed her hair aside. Her eyes flared emerald green. "Please, honey," she hissed. "Please, my Jackie...." she hissed, wiping spit from her mouth and smiling at me through green fire.

As if we were playing a game, I thought. The words skimmed across my thoughts and quickly disappeared.

Again, she lunged at my cock. I grabbed her hair and yanked her to the side. She groaned and I slapped her face.

Twice.

Hard.

She glared and smiled and squirmed in my grip. Her body convulsed and she attacked her tits and pussy as if she wanted to rip them off her body.

"Come on, Jackie," she said without focus, thrusting her body at me. "Please, honey. Please...."

I had to get the hell out of there.

I threw her back on the bed, climbed on top her, and slammed my cock into her. She cried out in obvious pain and delight and immediately thrust her hips up into me. I shoved her body down into the bed and pounded my cock into her as hard as I could.

Tears poured out of her. She sobbed and grunted, cried out and snarled. "Hard, hard, hard, hard," she mumbled over and over again.

My cock burned into her, aching and throbbing and sending ribbons of pain up my body. I couldn't stop.

I couldn't stop fucking her.

I couldn't stop and I couldn't cum.

She cried openly now and collapsed under me, mumbling, "Yes, yes, yes, yes," to something or someone inside herself.

I hammered my body against her, trying to hurt her more with every thrust. I saw myself, watched myself and cried out in horror at myself until unbearable pain ripped my cock out of her. I shivered, knelt back and struggled for breath.

She shook and curled into a ball, crying, squirming, babbling about how much she loved me and assorted gibberish I couldn't understand.

My cock throbbed and ached, unable to ejaculate, unable to soften. She saw me then, through muddy eyes, and twisted her body to get at me. She gently kissed my cock, massaged, licked and softly sucked on me. "Thank you, Jackie," she whispered without looking up at me. "You make me so happy."

Happy?

Happy?

My heart slowed and my breath collected itself. I watched her suck my cock like a twisted combination of child, whore and monster. Suddenly, from nowhere, I exploded in her mouth. She gagged and struggled and swallowed me whole. Again, she curled into herself and mumbled something unintelligible.

I knelt over her and let the pain wash over me.

I had to get the hell out of there.

And I did.

I dressed, keeping one eye on her. She ignored me, remained curled and slowly settled into a normal breathing rate. I stood and watched her ignore me, then left her there wrapped in her own knots.

My own room, for an instant, looked unrecognizable, as if everything I saw, everything I touched was all a dream that never existed. I fumbled for my wallet and keys on my dresser, looked at my stereo, my guitar, my bed, the posters, all of it unfamiliar now, unknown.

I passed her room on the way out and saw her unmoved, curled, sleeping, dead, I had no idea.

Next thing I was driving down the dirt road away from the house. Driving somewhere, going somewhere, something. I couldn't remember actually leaving the house, getting in the car, starting the engine.

After a mile I pulled over to the side of the road and turned off the engine.

Springtime.

A warm spring day, I noted as if making a list for survival. I rolled down the window and found myself shocked by the sound of nature. New birds, wind through the tall weeds, a distant tractor, pale yellows and greens waking up in slow motion.

What the hell was I doing?

What the hell just happened?

Over and over I asked myself until the words meant nothing and finally faded.

The quiet sounds of a fresh morning left me little defense against their calming effect. Fresh earth poured into my lungs. Fresh life poured into me, flushing my body with new energy.

I wasn't going back there, I decided, again feeling my heart rate increase at the thought.

And again, sweet green earth brought me back.

Sit, I told myself. Just sit. I focused on individual things, the rocks in the road, individual blades of grass, the cycling sway of the field. I examined the faint dust on my windshield and followed the lines left by my wiper blades.

I focused on the fine pattern of vinyl on my dashboard; the worn knobs on my radio. My weight pressed down on the seat. My feet rested flat on the floorboard. I knew I would return to her, I just didn't want to admit it to myself yet.

Not yet, I told myself. Not yet. Just sit here. Just sit here a moment.

I sat and thought nothing, judged nothing, felt nothing, requiring no effort to push anything and everything away. The need for motion fell upon me, and I started the engine, instantly losing the connection to my natural surroundings.

Motion.

I needed motion.

I had fucked her like a dirty piece of shit whore and I loved it –

No –

Stop.

Yes.

Drive.

I should go back –

No.

Stop.

Drive.

I put the car in gear and wondered if I could leave myself behind if I drove far enough –

She was my mother.

No.

Dirty whore.

No.

I drove, keeping to the back roads, concentrating on the sound of gravel under my tires.

I loved her.

No.

I made her happy.

No.

Fuck.

Drive.

I listened to the gravel ping off my car's body and drove faster.

I sought relaxation and surprisingly found it. So easy, I thought, to push it all away as odd photos and scrolling pictures I could simply ignore.

Me, not me, and so what, really? So what, all of it? The world hadn't ended, and wouldn't end because I fucked my mother. Just enough of it, maybe – and stop making such a big deal out of it. So what about any of it? So what? Just no more, and no more talking about it, thinking about it, feeling it, seeing it constantly roll across my mind.

No harm done, really.

A little strange, or a lot strange, but over now. Just over, and I could live there, be there, just fine.

Phrases and images hit me from odd angles, indecisive, unclear, pelting me from everywhere and forming sweet simple thoughts, teaching me not to overreact.

And that's all it was, really: Overreaction.

Yes, yes, yes, all of it, but not right now, not now because I drove and gravel slowly ruined my car's paint job.

I found myself in Dave's driveway, but I didn't remember turning on to any paved roads. Even after turning off the engine, the mild sound of gravel on paint sang in my ears.

Only after I knocked did I realize the house stood dark and quiet. The immediate squeak of the floorboards relieved me. The outline of Dave's mother through the curtained door window startled me. She wore a big puffy robe, big puffy slippers and she looked like everyone's mother.

Almost everyone. Mrs. Dixon peeked out, smiled and opened the door. She always smiled, always welcomed us no matter what time it was or what condition we were in. Hers was the house we could all crash at and escape to without judgment. Her home was our sanctuary.

God fucking bless her.

"Jack," she said, opening the door and stepping back for me to enter. She kept her voice down and carried a natural smile. "It's early. You okay, honey?"

"Yeah," I lied. "Hi. Hey, Miss Carol, I was just hoping to see Dave for a few minutes."

She'd been divorced a long time, since Dave and I were little. Dave, his older sister Katie and their mom all rolled into the first comfortable thought I'd had all day. Her house breathed good vibes.

"He's still sleeping," Miss Carol replied, turning toward the staircase door. "I think he's only been home a few hours. You didn't see him last night?"

"Ah, no, I had to help my mom with some stuff last night."

Miss Carol nodded and smiled and studied me for a moment. "You sure you're okay, Jackie?"

My breath shortened inside and I forced a smile. Only my mom and Miss Carol ever called me Jackie. "I'm just tired, too, I guess."

She nodded and didn't believe me. Miss Carol was old – not as old as my – as the – she was like forty-five or something – and she was one of us, though, our protector of sorts, our confidante.

Confidante in most ways, anyway.

"You can go see if you can wake him up," she said, and I felt as if I missed something else she'd said. I offered a bit of a smile and headed for the staircase door.

"When you want to talk, Jack," she said as I reached for the knob. "I'm here, you know."

I hesitated and almost blurted everything out.

I felt every bit of the cold brass knob as the fainted shiver crossed my palm. I didn't turn to look at her. I couldn't turn to look at her.

"Yes, Miss Carol," I said quietly. Every nuance of the old door mechanism vibrated my hand. I felt the knob twist, the latch slide and the final click of mechanical salvation straight into my heart. "I know."

I put a foot on the first step and finally managed to face her. I blurted, "Thank you," and froze for an instant. She hadn't moved and still offered her ever-present smile. Her wide mouth and clear, dark eyes threatened to release me.

I would explode into a million pieces if I didn't turn away. End it right here, I told myself, with Miss Carol of all people. She was the perfect person – or should have been the perfect person – in the perfect moment to – what? To save me? To tell me I shouldn't go home and fuck my mother again? To tell me it was alright that I had fucked her already, that I was alright, that everything was going to be alright?

Something inside me said, "Yes," to all of the above.

Instead, I said, "I will," and felt the lie burn like acid in my stomach. I felt her sigh as I turned away from her ever-present, now fading smile.

I stepped lightly up the stairs, desperate to keep the old farmhouse from creaking. The top of the stairs held only a platform large enough to choose one of three small bedrooms. Katie's room directly in front of me, the largest room, then the vacant room to my right, and Dave's room to my left.

I opened Dave's door without hesitation and stepped inside. He snored in the shadows and the room felt thick with sleep. I gently pushed the door closed until I heard a single click.

"Dave," I said, finding the strength of my voice awkward in the setting.

Nothing.

"Dave."

I looked at him from ten feet away, bunched in the covers and motionless. I watched him sleep in the dim room and decided not to wake him. For What? A joint? Money? What other reason could I give him?

Hey, Dave, I just fucked the shit out of my mother and I'm kinda freaked out.

Nope.

I thought of his mom. I *could* talk to her about it, I knew. She was exactly the person we could all talk to about anything. Perfect timing and the perfect moment, I thought again, with Dave and Katie both crashed out.

Yes.

No.

No fucking way.

I exited quietly and headed straight for the front door.

"Didn't want to wake him, huh?" Miss Carol blindsided me from the kitchen. "You sure you're alright?" she asked again, unable to let her perception slide.

"Yes," I said, and again I hesitated, this time with my hand on the front door knob. No, I thought. I didn't know what to say or how to say it. I didn't know where to begin or how to begin, and I felt like little more than a fool.

"Yes," I repeated, twisting the knob but still not opening the door.

"No one has to know what you tell me," she said out of nowhere, raising the hair on my neck and setting my stomach sideways. "Just between us, okay? You can even call me Caroline, if it helps."

"Caroline," I said quietly, stealing a quick glance at her eyes. A breath escaped me, then, "Maybe," I said, looking away. "I don't know."

My hand shook and the door opened.

Miss Carol nodded and released her invisible hold on me. "We'll just leave it open, okay? You want me to tell Dave you were here?"

"No," I said too quickly. I forced a smile and thanked her.

She smiled and said nothing as I poured myself out into the morning air. Breakfast, I thought. I could kill time with breakfast.

I saw my hand twist the ignition, heard the engine come to life, felt the gears engage and the car move. I went through all the proper motions and eventually sat staring at a plate of eggs and bacon, wondering where I was and how I was ever going to find a way back home.

Chapter 4

More headache than high, I sat in the driveway and stared like an idiot at the garage door. My escape had lasted little more than twelve hours. Now I found myself in the car in the dark with a pipe full of bowel-scraped resin. I flicked my lighter and drew a small breath, watching the black tar glow like charcoal and feeling my stomach twist into knots.

Over the last few hours my anger had shifted to Dad. He knew the bitch was crazy. He had to know. Selective blindness. Love. No one could be that stupid to be married to a lunatic and not know.

And he'd left me alone with her.

Coward.

Fuck the names, I thought.

Sissy fuck.

I drew another hit, coughed, gagged, winced and dumped the smoldering black chunks into the ashtray. What a bunch of shit, all of it, I thought. I considered sleeping in the car. Early spring and evening temperatures dropped like a rock. I shivered once, twice and still refused to start my engine.

The farmers must think we're idiots, I thought absently, staring into night. All of us nestled around and bunched together on our precious little five acre parcels. For what? And why did I suddenly give a shit?

I fumbled with the keys in the ignition and rolled the window half down, ignoring the cold. I lit a cigarette and wondered why we moved to the middle of nowhere when Dad's business was forty miles south on the edge of the city –

And who cared? I just wanted to know what version of reality was she going to be in when I went inside? I flicked my half-smoked cigarette into the yard and cut through the garage. Stuff, I noticed as if for the first time.

Motorcycles, snow mobiles, heavy duty garden tractor, tools, everything required to conquer the great outdoors. Dad even had a tractor from the 1940's set up to plow our third-mile long driveway.

Life on the edge.

I stopped at the door to the house and drew a breath. Again, I struggled with the notion of not coming home, not stepping through that door. I was old enough to drop out of school. I could just go.

Somewhere.

I could just *go.*

Cowardice may not be a sin but it was certainly a heavy blanket to carry around.

I twisted the knob and stepped into a dark house. I hadn't noticed every light in the house turned off when I drove up. I felt the weight of darkness, of her, in every breath. I stepped inside the door and listened.

I stood in the same spot where she'd sucked my cock and listened closer.

Nothing.

Her car was in the garage. She had to be home. She was here, somewhere. I could feel her heat, the bitch.

Bitch, I thought. *Whore.* The only names I could fasten to her. *Where the hell was she, and why the fuck was I here?*

My eyes wandered and adjusted and found nothing. I heard nothing except the mechanics of the house. I walked slowly through the dining area, around the kitchen and toward my room down the hall.

I stopped at her room and looked through the open door. The messy, exploding bed looked just like I left it, except she was gone.

She was just a bitch, I told myself, surprised at how easily I slipped her into the role. *Mother as whore.* She wasn't my mother, not like that, and whatever she was or wasn't, she wasn't in the room.

Maybe someone came over and took her out, I thought, going to my room. I took off my jacket and began emptying my pockets. Maybe Dad came over and got her and they were out reconciling. I didn't turn the light on and again found the room strangely unfamiliar, as if it had been stripped from me, as if I were simply a visitor, a passerby.

I'd lost this room somehow, as a part of me, as a teenage sanctuary of sorts. There was no sense of protection here any longer and no means of escape.

"Where'd you go, Jackie?" her voice came soft behind me.

I didn't turn around. Her inflection, tone, emotion, degree of presence – all of it told me who she was, and wasn't.

"I was afraid you weren't coming home," she said in a petulant manner.

"I'm home," I said, fumbling with my keys and wallet on the dresser. I didn't want to turn around. I didn't want to see her.

"Where else would I go," I said without asking.

I felt her take a step or two into my room, stealing more of my space from me. "Jackie, I'm sorry," she said, and for an instant she meant it. In that sentence I heard my mother's voice. "I'm so sorry, Jackie."

I looked up and found her standing barefoot, arms wrapped around herself, hair pulled back. She looked so small, so very small. She wore a brightly colored summer dress and seemed entirely out of place. Despite the trouble and pain inside, her image stood bright and she lit up the room.

I saw her as a woman, as a beautiful woman, despite her being almost sixty years old. I imagined her youth, the radiance of her, the presence of her. I knew then I had lost her as a mother, regardless of future events. As I had lost my father to business, I had lost my mother to sex. Nothing could get it back, in either case.

I hated them both.

And myself for accepting my role in their madness.

"Jackie, please," she begged, nervously stepping forward and stealing even more space. "I'm sorry."

I sighed, slumped and opened enough to let her come in and hug me. "We can't do that anymore," I said like a fool, letting her body push into mine.

"No," she agreed into my chest. She squeezed me and ran her hands up my back. "I'm so sorry," she said again with soft sincerity.

My hands slid down her back and felt no bra. I slid my hands to her waist, to the top of her ass and pulled her tight. Her large soft tits crushed against my chest and I felt her tears.

My cock stiffened and pressed against her. Panic grew and she held me in place with her eyes. She rubbed my neck and whispered, "It's alright, my Jackie," up into my ear.

No, I thought, unable to release her. No, it wasn't alright.

I stood back and pried her arms from around my neck. I tried desperately to call her Mother, to call her anything except bitch and whore.

She looked at me through darkness and pulled me close.

"Bitch," I said and failed to drive her away.

She kissed me on the lips and I kissed her back, tasting her, feeling my body pour into hers.

I pulled back and she pulled me forward. Our fingers barely touched, yet energy shot through my body and magnetized me in place. I felt every inch of her, every part of her wrap around and draw me in.

"This isn't alright," I said to anyone who would listen. Anger flared and drained just as quickly.

She was on my bed, then, somehow, hand fumbling in her dress pocket, dress up to her waist, legs spread and me upon her, inside her.

I fucked her, or was fucking her, or somehow I ended up on my bed, surrendering the last of my space to her. I missed all the steps in between and thrust into her, opening every part of her, feeling every part of her inside and out, watching her stretch and relax, her hands upon me, her legs around me.

Familiar hell, I thought in a daze, pushing her thighs apart and driving harder, fighting to find a connection. Everything about this felt familiar, as if I had done this before, as if we had done this a thousand times before, as if this one connection meant everything forever.

"Thank you," she said plainly in my ear, writhing like a snake around me. Her eyes flared chemical green and she hissed and pumped herself harder, forcing me to fuck like a maniac, I don't know, I didn't know what to do, what else to do.

"I love you so much, Jackie."

What the hell was she talking about?

Love.

"You're so good to me, so precious to me." She grunted between thrusts and spat the words at me like venom. Her body convulsed and released and covered me. Words exploded in my brain.

Had I done this before? Was all this a dream? Was any of this even happening? Was I really here, now, fucking my mother on my bed?

I looked down and almost puked. She lay spread and dripping, rubbing her swollen, wet pussy. I hung over her and watched her squirm and smile at me. She displayed herself for me as she rubbed our juices all over her body.

Her lips moved, but I couldn't connect the voice in my head telling me over and over again how happy she was, how pleased she was, with me, with us. Images of her flashed across my mind. I saw her there in a thousand different poses, in a thousand different outfits, in a thousand different renditions of the same story.

I pushed off the bed and finished removing my pants. She was off the bed, rubbing my neck, and telling me it was alright, telling me everything was alright and I was so good to her, and she was so happy, and everything was so damn perfect, how we'd be fine together, how we didn't need my dad, how I could do anything I wanted now, go anywhere, and always have a home here with her.

I slapped her face.

She didn't flinch.

"Shut up, bitch," I hissed and slapped her again.

She kissed me on the lips and I didn't flinch. I didn't back up. I kissed her back and hated everything. "Just shut up."

She nodded furiously, patting my arm and following me down the hallway like a pet. I could tell she wanted to keep talking, to keep babbling and prattling on. She wanted to know what I was doing, where I was going, if I was going to leave her for hours again. She wanted to know everything, what to do, how to act, what to say, what to wear –

Breathe.

But she knew not to say another word.

She knew enough to leave it open. She could do no more, she knew, and I felt it inside her. She opened and exposed herself fully, and fully expected the results to go in her favor.

Wicked, nasty bitch. I slammed my hand against the wall and hung still for a minute. I felt her a few feet behind me, tense, waiting, knowing her claws had sunk in deep.

I had to get the hell out of here, a familiar voice all but faded away.

My hard cock drilled into her and she was on the dining room table. I had put her there, I knew, thrown her up there. But it wasn't me, or was, and it didn't matter anyway. It was *my* cock blazing away inside her, stretching her open and ripping her apart.

The whore shook and braced herself against my deep, quick thrusts. She held herself open as best she could and I laughed when her head lolled like a rag doll. I plowed and pumped her, almost immediately spewed cum in and on her.

I slapped her, pulled out and staggered back.

She took the hit with an emerald stare and kept her legs apart and did everything she could to keep the invitation open.

Horrid, sick, bitch. I staggered into the living room and slumped into Dad's chair. What was I doing? Why couldn't I just get up and leave? Why couldn't I just get up and get the hell away from her?

She knelt and said things to me. Words rolled out of her and filled my brain with nonsense. I didn't know what she was saying, what she was talking about.

I ignored her. I wanted to beat her, hug her, kiss her, fuck her, and punch her in the face until she died. I ignored her until she went away. Sleep pulled me down into a black hole, crushing my body and mind to dust.

I dreamt of love and I woke in the dark with every muscle screaming. I didn't remember specific images, but I remembered the dream. The quiet comfort softened my muscles and held my soul as I staggered down the hallway and climbed into bed with my mother.

Chapter 5

Sunday and I had homework, I knew, and school tomorrow, and work in the afternoon with Dad. I wanted to keep putting my cock into the bitch, into the whore who was my mother, but by noon I had to get out of bed. She slept loudly and sprawled naked and messy across the sheets.

I stood over her and studied every wrinkle, every inch of her sagging body. My cock hung limp and pained between my legs. I felt drained and exhausted, disgusting and filthy, and I could do nothing to wash the sickness away.

So I lit one of her cigarettes, stood over her and pushed every question aside. This would not last, I told myself, blowing smoke over her. The sheer absurdity of our relationship could not sustain itself. Nature would not let it continue, I told myself. God would not let this continue.

So I told myself.

I stood in the shower and felt surprisingly better. I wouldn't have to do anything about it, I reminded myself. Everything would take care of itself. Everything was past now, and what was done, was done. I proclaimed to myself there would be no more insanity between us. I would call her Mom and forget the whole thing.

No harm done.

She would be Mom again and the thing with her and Dad would resolve itself to everyone's benefit. I couldn't fight any more, resist it, scream at it, rail against it.

I had done nothing wrong.

I had done nothing wrong, and it was over now.

Done.

Finished.

I scrubbed and watched the soapy water swirl down the drain. Invasions came and went. Images, yes, but feelings, too, in my body – *inside* my body. Sweeter language did not apply: I'd fucked my mother as hard as I could, as often as I could and I pumped as much cum into her as I could.

But it was over now.

Finished. And she would wake and agree.

She would feel as I felt and there would be no need to speak of it again.

Could, should, would, big fucking deal.

No.

Not like that, not like *big fucking deal*. Everything was fucked up, yes, but it was over now.

Just calm the fuck down.

I had homework and school work, and I lived here and everything was okay. Dad left and that was okay. Whether he came back or not, it was okay.

Nothing mattered, not really, and I just had to calm the fuck down.

The water swirled clear and I had nothing left to clean.

I dried myself and realized I hadn't gotten fresh clothes. Happiness flowed over me and I refused to fight the feeling. Confusion and horror rolled back and forth like an evening tide, and I felt foolish and artificial. Sex, that was it, just sex. Not that I'd had a bunch of it, sex, but it was just sex. I fucked her, yes. I fucked my mother. Yes.

I had done nothing wrong.

I stood naked in the hallway and found her sitting up naked in bed, disheveled, messy, exhausted and looking entirely her fifty-seven years. She smoked and watched me through olive drab eyes, waiting for a signal on how to greet the day.

I smiled and tossed my bathroom towel back into the bathroom. "I have homework," I announced with determination. Yet I could not call her *Mom*.

She hugged her knees up to her tits and pinched her ripe, swollen cunt out from between her thighs. Yet she didn't say a thing.

Cunt, I thought, enjoying the perfect word for her.

She smiled nervously and still said nothing. She wrapped herself tighter and rendered herself unreadable.

No matter. She was a whore and she would come to understand things were fine between us. She was my mother and she was a whore.

Simple enough.

I turned and escaped into my room for clothes.

"Do you want breakfast?" she called after me. I heard the uncertainty in her voice and I smiled as I dressed. Stupid bitch, I thought without cruelty or disdain. She will understand soon enough.

"Yes," I called back, sliding into jeans and a t-shirt. "I have to do my homework," I said, determined to conjure truth from repetition.

I sat at my small corner desk and ignored the discomfort of the situation. I didn't know what I was supposed to do or who I was supposed to be. Was I a high school student now? Was that what I was supposed to be right now?

Everything will work out –

Everything was already worked out –

Motherfucker.

Voices and foolishness filled my thoughts from every direction. My sore cock lay uncomfortably limp in my pants as I reached for my algebra book.

I told myself I studied and I genuinely scoured the pages of the book until frying bacon commanded my attention. Everything felt light in the air, as if substance no longer applied to anything. The room, the desk, the chair I sat in to the air I breathed all felt equally insubstantial.

Everything was a dream, I told myself. Everything was a dream if I let it be – or if I let myself simply marvel at the perpetual, perverted smile inside my mind. I resisted nothing and flipped algebra pages back and forth, viewing the same problems over and over, absorbing and understanding nothing.

I blinked and reached for my cigarettes and ashtray.

There was no ashtray and I called and said as much to my, to the, to her, to my bitch.

Whore, I thought.

Both of us.

She appeared behind me and gently set a clean ashtray down. Awkwardness slid between us for an instant, and I wondered if she felt it, if she could grab on to it and pull herself to sanity – pull us both to sanity. But she simply squeezed my shoulder and told me breakfast would be ready shortly.

She kissed my temple quickly, as a good mother would and left me in peace. She was beginning to understand, I told myself without evidence. She was fine, and everything was fine, I told myself, as I watched my hand write algebraic equations.

She sat naked beneath a thin silk robe as we ate. Prepared for anything, I supposed, and as uncertain as I of our roles together. I felt sorry for her in a strange way. She would never be my mother again. Much like Dad turning into my boss and taking a slice of family connection with him, Mom turned into my whore and abandoned everything of herself, of her family, overnight. The sudden complexity of it, of her, startled me as I ate.

But, I could not simply discard her as a used up whore, and I knew I had to say something. I loved her then, as someone unrecognizable and undefined. *Things must fit quickly*, I decided, or we would each drown in misunderstanding and fear.

I put my fork down and leaned over to her. She reflexively leaned toward me and I kissed her softly on the lips. I discarded the awkward moment and reveled in her brief, if somewhat confused, smile.

"I'm not going anywhere," I said then, too rapidly. I told her we'd be alright and made the air thick with confusion and misunderstanding.

I sighed and looked away. Jane, her name, simply didn't roll off my lips. "I don't want to call you a whore," I heard myself say so easily. "I don't want to call you a bitch."

She looked at me with a surprising amount of understanding. I wasn't sure what she thought she understood, but I accepted her openness as willingness to appreciate my position.

"I can't call you 'Mom' ", I said, listening to myself talk and following the words without exception. "I can't call you 'Jane', either."

She nodded without expression and turned toward her plate. She folded in on herself and I couldn't keep my eyes off her. She flinched under the pressure and I loved her again in an odd, wordless way. I wanted something written down in a book, some definition, some method of understanding what I felt.

"I fucked you like a whore last night," I said, surprised at my blunt delivery. "Isn't that crazy I don't want to call my mother a whore?"

She squirmed in her chair, then looked up quickly as if she had something to say. Then just as quickly went back to picking at her food.

"I don't understand, Jack –"

"There isn't –"

"You're calling me a whore," she said, ignoring my interruption and looking up with tears in her eyes. "You say you don't want to call me a whore, but you're calling me one right now."

Her hands shook over her plate and she set her fork down and folded her hands in her lap. "I'm still your mother," she said to her plate.

No, I thought, reaching across the table and squeezing her shoulder and neck. She cried openly, nervously. I sighed and slid her chair along with her over to me. She wrapped her arms around my neck and cried herself out.

"You're a whore and I love you," I said, petting her like a child. Realization set in, I imagined, and she cried herself through acceptance.

"I'm so sorry, Jack," she whispered in my neck, and I didn't understand her pain. "I love you," she said, distorted in confusion, and we kissed, misunderstanding everything and struggling for survival.

Stupid whore, I thought, pushing her robe open and rubbing her bare hips and thighs.

She spread and slid closer to me, lifting her leg and making herself immediately available.

"I love you, too," I said, not fully integrated yet and I released her.

She sat back and pushed her hair aside, immediately aware of her appearance.

"I have to finish my homework," I said again, pushing myself up and standing above her. She fumbled with her hair as if she'd been caught by the devil with her hand in the fire. "The dress you had on yesterday was nice," I added, marveling and searching for the source of my words.

She nodded and stood without looking at me. She hurriedly gathered the dishes and scrambled for the kitchen.

I frittered away and listened to her shower, listened to her dress, apply makeup, and beautify herself for what seem an eternity. I sensed her presence, her movement, her every motion in every place she went. I heard her breathe from the other side of the house.

A sudden rush of open, raw fear washed over me and I panicked for a moment. The real sensation persisted and again I felt myself drift.

Truth, something said and a shiver ran down my spine. I put down my pencil and felt the sensation this time in my hands. A tingling, vibrating, illusory sensation traveled across my skin. The rushing desire to leave, to get up, get in my car and drive away flooded every part of me.

I struggled and forced myself back in the chair. Sore eyes showed I'd done nothing except doodle on a piece of paper for the last hour.

She came into my room and saved me, the bitch. Her red-gray hair flowed down to her shoulders. Spiral green eyes deep with mascara and eye liner. She stood in front of me and smiled warmly, spun around slowly for me and lifted her dress to show me her gray-haired cunt.

I smiled and fear sizzled inside, burning away inside and stiffening my cock. I nodded my approval, then dismissed her with a turn.

I caught her smile and felt her happiness and joy throughout the house as she began to clean. I failed continuously at my homework. I watched her round ass shake as she moved about her day. We ate lunch in silence, I named her nothing and by early evening I'd long given up on algebra.

She sucked my cock that night and told me she loved the taste of my cum. I made her happy, she told me over and over again in countless variations. I fucked her twice before we fell asleep in each others arms.

I woke late for school, leaving her sleep while I dressed and hurried out the door.

The air of familiarity returned when I stepped out into the fresh morning air. I hesitated and felt I'd been here before, seen all this, felt all of it, whatever it was, as if I lived someone else's used and discarded life.

The bizarre sensation drifted around me as I drove toward school and never arrived. I couldn't name it right or wrong, the sex, the suddenness of it – and the bullshit of it, because I knew it wouldn't last.

We needed this right now, I told myself as I drove past the school and headed toward the mall. We needed this, the bitch and I, and it would be over soon enough.

She would be fine. She was okay. Once it got out of her system she would be fine.

No harm done.

Chapter 6

I showed up early to Dad's shop, lied about getting off school early and stood in front of his desk, waiting.

"Jack, I don't know," he said without looking up, without looking at me. "Clean the shop, make some drive cleats or something. I'll pay you for the rest of the day."

Dismissed.

"Dad," I started, then immediately stopped. Okay then.

Okay. Drive cleats and assorted sheet metal bullshit it was.

He knew why I stood there, though, so I hesitated just a fraction of a fuck you. He'd had all weekend to think of something to say, anything to say. I spent the weekend fucking his wife, my mother, in a bizarre attempt at sanity, and I felt like he owed me a goddamn explanation.

He could have come up with at least some bullshit reason why he left.

Instead, nothing.

So I grabbed the broom and cleaned the already clean shop. He just had to muster it up and spit it out. He had to come to terms with *it* while *it* stood in his face.

Constant tension spilled readily between us. He had to say something to me about his leaving and he hated explaining anything to anyone. I swung the broom through the motions and told myself it didn't matter. I was everyone's whore.

Yes, fuck you, I was everyone's whore.

My hands shook to the point I almost dropped the broom. I stood baffled in an empty shop, shamed by my sudden insight.

No. I made it all sound wrong. Where was I supposed to go? I was supposed to go to school and graduate. I was supposed to smoke dope and fuck the neighbor's daughter, not my own goddamned mother.

Stop, I thought. Stop damning everything. I'd fucked myself raw and went to work in Dad's shop. But no, not like that. I searched for yesterday's reasoning and found only absent scribbling on unfinished homework. This morning, I had driven right past school.

I made too much of it all.

Sweep Dad's floor, fuck Mom's cunt. What difference did it make?

Come on, I thought, I set the broom down and had to get the hell of the shop. I had to get the hell out of there.

What now?

What now what now what now?

Miss Carol's face flashed across my eyes and the door behind me opened, shattering the vision of her face into a million shards of laughter. *Yeah,* I thought, and turned around to face my dad. *I could tell Miss Carol all about fucking my mom.*

"Jack," Dad began, lighting a cigarette and preparing to spew bullshit. "I don't know what your mother told you –"

"Nothing," I replied too quickly. *She couldn't speak very well with my cock in her mouth.* I drew a breath and said calmly, "She didn't say anything except you split up. You moved out."

I shrugged and left it hang. I didn't give a shit anymore, at least this minute. Whores didn't give a shit. I looked at my dad and saw the shame and humiliation I felt in my heart. I wanted to punch him in the face so I gave him an out.

Asshole.

"Dad, just don't worry about it. I just don't understand. I don't know where you live, or your phone number, or anything." I stopped and shrugged again, stood and stared.

He dug in his pocket and pulled out a crumpled piece of paper. "This is my address," he said, offering me the folded mess. "My phone number. You can call me anytime you want, Jack," he said, appearing to finally notice the strangeness of the conversation. He'd left me too he realized – or I told myself he realized. Either way.

I looked at his paper mess and felt tears inside. *Dad,* I thought. *Why are you doing this?*

I blurted, "It's an apartment?" and other nonsense, suddenly desperate to share words, thoughts, anything to hear his voice.

He nodded, nervous now and quiet. "Lakeside Township," he said as an after thought.

"Lakeside Township," I repeated. "We did some jobs there. By the water?"

"No. Yeah," he stumbled. "I don't live by the water."

He wanted to say more, or I wanted him to want to, but I couldn't tell and it really didn't matter. Maybe something else, I didn't know, and we were both way out of character.

"Maybe I could come over some time and see it." I lit another cigarette. We stood by the dumpster and I thought about the last time I saw him, when he had already left and I still didn't know.

He shrugged and I told myself it didn't matter. "It's not much, Jack," he said. I heard the strain in his voice. He approached the end of the conversation. "We'll go see a movie or something," he added, correcting the tone of his voice.

I nodded and missed him, of all things. I missed him as a father, as my dad, something we hadn't had in years. I would have to go to dinner with him, now. We would go to dinner, the movies and make scheduled visits, like appointments.

He was gone. He stood right in front of me and was gone. I thought of Mom and didn't call her a bitch or a whore.

"I gotta go inside and make some calls," he said as if apologizing. "You can go if you want. I'll pay you for the day."

I nodded and didn't want to leave. I was afraid to leave. I couldn't go home, not yet, not this early. Barely two in the afternoon and I'd be home by three –

He gave me a hug then, my dad – and I did everything to keep tears back. I wanted him to come home with me, to help mom, to help all of us, to keep everything normal, to return everything back to whatever version of normal he wanted.

Not like this, I thought, hugging him back. "Maybe we can go to a movie Friday or something," I said without thinking, yet reaching and grabbing at anything.

"Yeah," he said. "We sure can, Jack." He straightened up and told me it would be alright and then he disappeared into the shop.

I squatted down behind the dumpster, threw up and cried. Shame, embarrassment, pride, hatred, love, lust, everything tore apart and reassembled in the wrong order, in no order at all. After a few minutes of self pity, I composed myself and sat in my car, deciding between Dave and Eddie. They were probably together, I reasoned, at Dave's house.

I craved something familiar and ignored the transition from city to county. I held my breath until I reached Dave's driveway.

"Where the hell you been?" Eddie Palzola said when I walked into Dave's house unannounced. "You look like shit." Both guys slumped on the couch and smiled up at me. *General Hospital* had just started and Luke and Laura already struggled to save the world. Eddie blew a long stream of smoke out of his mouth and passed the joint up to me.

"Fuck you" I replied and hit the joint, savoring every bit. I felt the immediate rush of the farmer's homegrown and collapsed into the big, worn out chair near the television. I looked from Dave to Eddie on the couch and laughed.

I held on to the joint and laughed my fucking ass off. I couldn't stop and didn't care. I shook and smoked and grabbed my stomach from the pain. Dave and Eddie stared at me, leaned forward and waited anxiously for the source of my insanity.

I'm fucking my mother, I screamed in my head. *My old man left and I'm putting the cock to his wife while he's away. She's a whore, my mother. I'm a whore. We're all whores.*

Eventually I stopped laughing.

I offered up the part about my dad leaving and told them it got better but I couldn't share the entire joke just yet.

"Ah, man, that sucks," Dave said, taking the joint back from me and passing it on.

"I'm going to the movies with him on Friday," I said. "Like a date."

"Shit," Eddie replied, slouching back down and turning to the television. He had a crush on Laura and couldn't keep his eyes off the television. "It sucks, man, but I dunno. I wish my parents would get a divorce."

Eddie was heavy Catholic-Italian and there was no divorce in his family. From what I saw the few times I'd been to his house, his life consisted of misunderstanding, contradiction and violence.

"That's why you weren't in school today, man," Dave said, nodding to himself as if understanding.

The conversation stopped there and the pressure built again.

Miss Carol wasn't home, which is why we blew pot smoke all over her living room. She worked as a nurse's aid in town and although she knew we all got high in her house she didn't like seeing the act performed live.

As if I would have talked to her anyway.

I couldn't imagine taking her up on her offer now. I couldn't do that to her, walk up to her and lay it all out for her, tell her what was going on. I couldn't imagine telling anyone I fucked my own mother – a bunch of times.

Shit.

The thought brought instant nausea. Acid boiled in my stomach and I thought I would vomit right then and there. I sat back in the chair and pretended to focus on the television.

I wondered what she was doing right now, the bitch. Cooking dinner for me? Anxious to suck my cock when I get home? My knee bounced at a maniacal pace until Dave and Eddie both stared at me.

"Arcade, dudes," Dave said, stretching and sitting up. "Let's go blast aliens and look at tits."

Eddie panicked and stared at him. "After General Hospital, man." Then he looked from Dave to me and my knee and nodded. "Yeah, man, okay...."

I barely noticed anything. Everything was different when I was with her. Why was it different when I was with her? Everything else, anything else, felt like a different world, an artificial world. Even my thoughts said different things, showed different pictures. I fought the urge to get up and leave, to race home to her. Why the hell would I want to do that? What the hell was the matter with me?

"Jack, come on...."

What?

I looked up and saw them standing and waiting.

The arcade, yes. I remembered something about an arcade and wandered outside behind them. I climbed into the backseat of Eddie's car and literally came unglued. I felt outside myself as if I shared the back seat with my body. One second, birds and wind through the trees; the same second the rush of wind through the open car window.

Dave sparked another joint as soon as we hit the road. I inhaled deeply as we sailed down the road at light speed. Good and bad, connected, disconnected, disgusted, turned on, hateful and loving everything and nothing, an exploding ball of raw emotions tumbled out of my flesh.

Pure exhaustion and energy flooded my body, ten times any adrenaline or drug rush I'd ever felt. Dave said something to Eddie about letting me be as I walked into the arcade behind them. I was so fucking high, so fucking happy and so fucking pissed off. I stalked the aisles while frantic bells and whistles hammered into my brain.

I stopped and watched a little kid pound away on *Defender*, my favorite game. And I laughed outrageously as his score blew past my own personal best. I gave him four quarters and told him to keep going.

I said something crude, something awful and distasteful to a young girl standing with her girlfriends. Someone slapped me and threatened to tell someone about something I couldn't remember. I laughed again and told them they missed out on some quarters.

I dropped a quarter in *Tempest* and lost it in a swirling, maddening flashing instant. I looked around for Dave and Eddie and found hordes of kids, chaotic lights and noise.

A lot of noise.

I remembered I hated noise and hated arcades and I laughed again, receiving and ignoring one strange look after another. *I had to go home*, I told myself, calm and correct inside. *I had to go home and do my duty, earn my keep.*

Keep Momma full of cum, I thought, feeling the incoming rush of a deep headache. I shoved a quarter into a game I'd never seen before and walked away without playing.

I didn't understand the big kid in front of me. Football jock, fuck, what the hell was he talking about his girlfriend for? Who the hell was he and why did I give a shit? And why didn't I give a shit? And what the hell, again, and why was I on the floor? Why did my face hurt? And why was everyone staring at me? I didn't recall dropping acid or taking a hit of mescaline.

"It was just fucking weed," I said, or thought I said. What the hell was wrong with everyone? Son of a bitch, I thought.

And I was.

Dave picked me up from the floor and Eddie yelled at the big kid. I didn't understand any of it.

I was truly the son of a bitch – my mother, the cocksucking whore – damnit my face hurt, and why was it so fucking cold outside?

"Fucking cold outside," I heard myself say.

"Damn, dude," Eddie said. "We gotta get outta here before the football team eats my car."

"Assholes," a part of me said without interest.

"What the hell did you say to him, Jack?"

"I dunno, I dunno," I said, trying to remember. "Something about fucking his girlfriend in the ass, I think."

We exploded in laughter and for a moment I felt right at home.

"Geezus," Dave said.

"I am fucked up," I declared. "In every way I am one sorry sonofabitch."

"Amen," Dave agreed.

Eddie smiled and said nothing as he drove us into the night, out of city lights and back into darkness.

Chapter 7

It wasn't that she didn't want it, or want to do it – the thought being a joke in itself – I just had a bit of a struggle coordinating the effort, or attack, or whatever it was called.

"Just keep this shit with you," I said to her, pushing her legs apart as she sat on the corner of the bed. I snatched the tube from her hand and read *KY Lubricant*. "Just keep this shit with you, even around the house."

"Yes, Jack," she replied in such a pale voice.

She was so dry, so damn dry – a dried up old hag without the shit in the tube. I couldn't shove my cock into her on the couch, so I had to drag her into the bedroom.

"Jackie...," she said once or twice as she scurried behind me, tripping and stumbling to hold my pace.

"Just keep it in your pocket or something," I said again, already tired of her or tired of something. My head pounded and throbbed as I shot the stuff into her and worked her open with two, three then four fingers without pause.

She grunted and mumbled something and seemed generally uncomfortable – which didn't stop her from pushing her bare feet against the floor and spreading her legs open. She scrambled for some kind of position, something to hold on to, I guessed. I stretched her cunt open and almost pushed my entire hand into her.

She gyrated in rhythm and bucked her hips, fucking my hand like a slow motion lunatic.

Without control, I thought, watching her perform. But she wasn't in control, either. So who was? My dad? Miss Carol? Dave? Eddie? Me? I watched her eyes darken and listened to her shallow, hungry breaths. Then I took advantage of us both and observed it all from the safety of my internal prison cell.

The instant I released her she fist-fucked her own cunt. I paused to watch because *Jesus-fucking-Christ*. I fumbled with my pants and couldn't take my eyes off her. I grabbed her ankles and yanked her close, then slammed my cock into her.

She went wild, or insane, or both.

She screamed and cried and bucked like an animal. She cursed at me in another language, I thought, and I pulled my cock completely out of her and slammed it back in, throwing us into furious, body slamming rhythm.

She jerked and humped and dug her fingernails into my neck. I leaned in, drove us faster and slapped her face.

Her eyes ignited with green fire. Her face twisted and distorted into a hideous mask. She bared her teeth and lunged to bite my arm. Her teeth hit with a loud, empty clack and she growled and tried again.

I ripped the sundress open and attacked her tits with my own claws. She swung and missed and growled like an animal in a trap. I twisted one of her nipples and bit into her flabby tit. She cupped her hand and nailed the side of my head, ringing my ear.

I climbed on top of her and attacked her cunt with every thrust. Her fingers dug into my head and she pulled me close, pulled me down to her, snarled something and pumped her hips into me.

I shivered and exploded inside her. Raw, electric pain ripped every muscle and forced every thought into chaos. She squirmed, twisted and kicked at me as I pulled away. I knocked her flailing limbs aside, picked her up under her arms and threw her against the head board.

She paused only an instant before attacking her cunt with her fingers. I stood back off the bed and watched her brutalize her own body. Her rabid green gaze held me until she shook from her own orgasm.

I shivered and walked out of the room. She scrambled after me like a dog and followed me into my bedroom. Raw, twisted emotion radiated out of her.

"I did some laundry," she said stupidly.

So what, you stupid bitch, I thought.

"I hung it up in the other closet."

I opened my closet and said nothing. She meant her closet. She meant Dad's side of the closet. I pretended not to care and flipped through my remaining clothes as if I paid attention to my actions.

"God," I said, or something similar. "Bitch."

"Jackie –"

"I can't call you 'Mom'," I said without turning around. "I told you that."

She hugged me from behind and squeezed my tense shoulders. I felt her warm cheek through my shirt and I stood there and let her hug, squeeze and capture me.

"Jackie, it's alright –"

"It's not alright," I snarled and twisted free. "What the hell is this? What the hell are we doing?"

She looked genuinely confused, as if we weren't doing anything out of anyone's ordinary routine.

I wanted to beat the living shit out of her. Instead, I exhausted myself on her blank, pale stare and told myself no one was this stupid.

"Fine," I said or sighed or something and pushed passed her toward her room. Stupid had nothing to do with it, I knew, and it didn't help anyway.

Again, she followed me like a dog. We stood naked in the dark on either side of the bed. Shadows lied and I saw the animal inside her reflect the animal inside me. I saw war and murderous rampage, torture, degradation and death. Then we both lit cigarettes and blew smoke at each other.

All of this was on me, I decided, watching her watch me. I had made every final move, present moment included. She simply presented herself and offered opportunity. I took it every time.

Damned if I didn't take what she offered every time.

She wouldn't say anything, I knew. Words interrupted her feelings. Words disrupted her flow. I knew nothing of her, really, her life before me and Dad. I found myself in bed next to her, preparing for sleep, with her head on my shoulder. She lay so I couldn't make eye contact with her. I touched her once and fell asleep.

Where was she, I dreamt, turning and finding her everywhere. Where was I, I dreamt, turning and finding her everywhere.

In the morning, I cooked breakfast and decided school could fuck off for two days in a row. Work was dead and I knew Dad wouldn't miss me.

But, why the day off?

I hated the question and hated my self examination. Day off to fuck your mother some more, the terrible little voice in my head screamed.

No.

No, fuck no. I beat the hell out of the eggs and tried not to think about myself standing naked in the kitchen. She needed strength, I told myself. She needed food and energy so I could fuck her some more.

I let the bacon sizzle and brought her a coffee. She lay sprawled out half under the covers, lightly snoring. I set the cup down and nudged her to no avail. I bent down and kissed her forehead and watched with mixed emotions as she woke with a smile.

"I'm making you breakfast," I said, awkwardly, nodding toward the coffee. "I'll bring it to you," I added with a measure of discomfort.

Then I'm going to fuck the shit out of you until you pass out.

I pushed everything aside and returned to the kitchen. Everybody went through this, or something like this, I told myself. No, not everybody fucked their mothers, but everybody had the crazy voices in their head. I knew they did.

I knew they did.

This is all normal for now, and I knew it, just for now.

Stupid shit, really.

She smiled and pushed up for a kiss. Old fucking hag. I kissed her quickly and let her fondle my cock.

"I love you, Jackie," she said with golden green eyes.

"I love you, too," I replied, tasting the awkward truth of the statement. I did love her. I hated her fucking guts, but I loved her more than anything I could imagine.

I cooked her breakfast and knew I had to decide one way or the other. I looked around the kitchen, waiting for the toast, and considered everything. Nice stuff, good quality shit. Dad never bought junk. I thought about the stuff in the garage, in the basement and wondered how it was all supposed to work out. He lived in an apartment – and I pictured him there and me here – and his bitch here, in his bed, drinking my coffee and getting ready to eat my food and suck my cock.

She thanked me for it every time.

Fuck him and her.

And fuck me, too. Whore assholes, the lot of us.

The toast popped and shook me awake. Wrong voices at the wrong time, I told myself. Stupid shit didn't matter anyway.

As if I was going to live here forever.

As if Dad wouldn't be coming home.

As if this wasn't just a stupid game – like stupid arcade games, burning up quarters and wasting time.

We ate and fucked and didn't get out of bed until five in the afternoon. She asked once about school, but didn't seem to give a shit about the answer. I got tired of her telling me how much she loved me and my cock, and how happy she was, and how this was the best day ever.

I listened to her bullshit and pumped her full of cum until I stood drained and dripping in the shower. I denied everything, shut down everything and soon found myself in the dining room.

She bounced and flitted around, cooking dinner, humming, smiling. She was absolutely gorgeous filled with my cum, and she looked at least twenty years younger. Her eyes glittered almost blue.

Who was I kidding? I loved her. I loved the way she looked and smiled at me. I loved the way I could walk up and touch her any way I wanted, anytime I wanted. I loved the way she cooked and cleaned and the way her tits hung in her dress. I loved the way her soft, round ass felt in my hands when I fucked her.

She was happy and so was I.

Only one frightened little asshole remained in my brain and kept my thoughts askew. Foolishness. She was too old for me, of course. And no one would understand, of course. But then, no one needed to understand. No one needed to know or understand anything.

I sat and stared and watched her serve me dinner. I didn't know what else to do – and I didn't want anything else to do. I was fine in my own skin, I told myself, ignoring fear and foolishness.

We ate in silence and spent the evening watching television. The last thing I remember was the sight of my clothes hanging in my dad's closet. Sleep fell like a dead black, dreamless thing.

In the morning, early summer storms began.

Chapter 8

"You're running out of excuses, Preston," Mr. Kowicki the student counselor said without looking at me.

Fuck you, I thought. "Yes, Sir," I said.

"You've got six weeks left of the year and only two absences left, Preston." He looked at me as if I were going to offer a revelation. The bald little man pushed his glasses up his nose and used silence as a weapon.

I thought about what to say.

I actually thought about my words. New ground, indeed.

"Mr. Kowicki, I've had some trouble at home that I'd rather not talk about. I know I've missed a lot of school in the last few weeks, but everything is getting back to normal. I don't intend to miss any more school."

I sat back, reasonably proud of myself.

Mr. Kowicki stared at me, pushed his glasses up his nose again and sighed. "Preston," he began, and for a moment he didn't seem to know where to take my name. He hesitated, looked down and rubbed the top of his head.

"Preston," he said as if he understood my lies. "Preston, I'm sorry if you've got trouble at home. But you've also got a 1.5 average in school. Even if you pass all your classes this year you won't have enough credits to graduate with your class."

I didn't give a shit.

"Summer school is the only way you'll be able to graduate on time."

Food, pussy, shelter, I thought. "I understand," I said, leaving it flat between us.

The last two weeks at home finally mellowed into the semblance of a twisted routine. I did not wish to disturb the calm hysteria that was my mother.

"What do you understand, Preston?" Kowicki asked.

Fuck you, I thought, and fuck this place. I had a good job – and a place to live, a cook, a maid and a whore. At seventeen years old, what else did I need?

Fuck you and your high school diploma.

I didn't say shit.

Kowicki sighed and sat back.

"Look, *Jack*," he said with his human voice. "If you've got problems at home, you have to tell someone. If you've got something troubling you, then you have to get it out in the open. It's perfectly normal to need to talk to someone now and then."

What the fuck did he know about my *normal*?

And what the fuck was normal, anyway?

What did he know about taking care of my mother, of *my* mother? And why the hell did he care, anyway?

"You want me to go to summer school, is that it," I asked without the question. "I don't know. I gotta think about it –"

"Jack," he said. I hated when he used my first name. "You won't graduate–"

"I get it," I said, abruptly getting out of my chair. "I gotta think about it."

I had to leave. I had to get the hell out of there, out of his cramped little bullshit office. "Can I go back to class now?"

He nodded and looked utterly exhausted.

I looked at the hallway clock and saw only ten minutes left of class. One more, I thought. One more lecture or whatever to sit through and I could get the hell out of there and go to work.

Fuck, I thought, opening my locker door for shelter.

Fuck.

Panic set in – again, and I couldn't find the source – again. My chest tightened, my heart raced and I felt as if I didn't run as far and as fast as I could my life would explode.

Except I had nowhere to run. I rattled off one excuse after another why I shouldn't just throw some clothes in my car and take off into the wild blue yonder.

Let her go insane. She was only a few steps away, as it was. Bitch.

Whore.

I would miss her.

One whore to another.

Blood raced through my veins. I looked up at the clock and saw six minutes to go. Would I miss her?

I called her Mom when I fucked her now, along with bitch and whore and a few others. I couldn't remember when all those words became interchangeable.

What the fuck was I doing?

One more class, I told myself. *Just one more class. Don't take an absence. Just go to class, go to work, go home.*

Home.

There was nothing easy about Mom's cunt: I made no mistake about that, at least.

Mom's cunt.

My wet palms slid down the locker door. I'd fucked my mother every day for the last two weeks.

That was insane.

I was insane.

I was a sick, insane motherfucker and I was going to go home and do it again.

I *wanted* to go home and do it again.

I only had a half day of actual school, the rest on work co-op and I couldn't manage to stay in school for three lousy classes.

I dismissed Kowicki and summer school without a second thought.

Dad was supposed to have moved back home by now. Two weeks, I thought. I glanced at the clock and saw three minutes left. He was supposed to have realized what a dumbass he was for leaving and come home by now. He was supposed to have come home and saved me from her.

But it didn't matter now, anyway, I thought. Would she even let him come home? And, what if he did?

"Here, Dad," I would say. *"Here's your bed, closet and whore back. I used them well and watch out for the sticky parts. Glad to have you back."*

Yeah.

This was stupid. Everything was stupid. School, Dad, Mom, me equals stupid. What difference did anything make? I was as big a whore as my mother and I was going to go home again and prove it.

And she'd thank me.

And I'd cut the lawn or some shit, and she'd cook, and we'd watch television, and I'd ignore Dave and Eddie's phone calls, and I'd fuck her again, and, and, and....

What was the fucking point?

We weren't hurting anyone. We weren't hurting each other, not really. Not really.

The bell rang and startled me. The hallway filled with motion and noise until I thought my temples would explode.

Mom was happy. She was so happy and funny and cheerful and sweet. I couldn't remember seeing her like that, like the whole package, ever. I couldn't remember seeing her so goddamn happy.

"*I love you so much, Jackie,*" she told me every day. "*I love your cock so much.*"

She believed it.

We both believed it.

Seeing was believing and living it was unbelievable.

I slammed my locker shut and wandered through the hallway, found the door to the parking lot and left. I just left and I couldn't stop shaking. I pulled over less than a mile from school and sat with my hand on the door handle, waiting to lean out and vomit.

Go home and cut the grass, I told myself. Five acres of rolling hills took the better part of a week to cut, meandering in between a zillion small trees, trying not to roll the garden tractor. I could disappear on the tractor for hours.

I drove home down the back roads and for twenty minutes I enjoyed the fresh spring air through my open windows. Fresh gravel, fresh earth. I burned through an entire joint and found myself exceedingly stoned by the time I hit the driveway.

My eyes burned when I pulled up to the garage and killed the engine. My brain literally spun and went numb. Thought slid into momentary flashes of nonsense interspersed with crude shots of recent memory.

I walked directly to the garage door opener. I filled the tractor with gas, checked the oil and smiled to myself about how well I adjusted to life without Dad. This wasn't so bad, really, I thought, climbing on the little green tractor and pulling the choke knob. I actually got shit done around here. Grass and shit, picking up the yard, straightening stuff, sorting and cleaning stuff. Plus, I was quite the good fuck, according to Mom anyway.

What a fucking sad joke.

And speak of the devil, the door to the house opened as soon as I hit the key. I saw the bitch wave frantically to me as the motor roared to life. I saw desperation on her face and in her mannerisms. She made it clear she wanted my attention.

I was in no condition to deal with her. *Relax, Mom, bitch, whore, whoever the fuck you are right now.* I clicked the tractor into reverse and pulled out of the garage.

"Later," I called out over the drone of the engine.

She took a step or two out of the garage and I thought she might chase me down the hill. She looked angry, still insisting on my attention.

I spun the steering wheel, shifted down and sped away from her, thankful the next section to cut was down by the road. *Go cook something and warm up your cunt.* I sped away and lit a cigarette. My buzz was just too good to waste on her, or anyone for that matter.

I turned around in the seat and saw her standing on top of the hill, hands on her hips as if she had authority. The sun dress thing was getting old, I thought absently, although I appreciated the accessibility.

Nothing that couldn't wait, I thought, dismissing her and turning around. I turned on the mower blades, swerved off the driveway and tore into the lawn. I laughed, coughed and shifted into a lower gear.

I swerved around and meandered between trees, pushed up under bushes and rolled up and down hills for hours. My buzz had long since ended, and evening chill set in, when I decided to call it quits on the lawn. I was hungry and out of gas, anyway.

Time for her, then. Yes. I shivered against the chill and saw the sun low on the horizon. I rattled up the driveway and decided if I could just stop freaking out like a sissy everything would work out fine.

Everything was fine, I told myself over and over as I parked the garden tractor. I fucked up at school, but I already knew more about heating and cooling than people ten years older than me. The rest of it was just bullshit anyway. Diplomas and college, fuck it. I was just acting stupid about everything else.

About her.

We weren't hurting anyone. I wasn't dating her and I certainly wasn't planning on living there forever. I had to stay until I could save enough money – and that was it: Just stay until I had enough cash.

I pictured her on the hill hours earlier. I drove the tractor into the garage and killed the motor. I imagined her in the future as I drove away and left her alone here.

Who would cut the grass? Who would plow the snow? Who would fix the stupid things like the plumbing and electrical in the house when they broke? I pictured her home alone at night, wrapped around herself in front of the television. She wouldn't cook for herself or keep the place clean, I imagined.

I climbed off the tractor and stretched the kinks out of my back. Mrs. Howard's house stood a few acres over. She'd taken Mom for her chemotherapy treatments a few years ago. The journey was something like four hours there and back and she took Mom three times a week. At a time when cancer still meant a social death sentence, Mrs. Howard was amazing.

So, what then? Let the neighbors take care of her?

I cursed my dad and opened the door to the smell of homemade Asian food. He would have to clean up his own mess sooner or later. Or not, I realized. He didn't have to do a damned thing.

I stood in the kitchen and washed up, looked around and didn't see her.

"The school called me, Jack," she said from behind, from somewhere. I almost jumped out of my skin.

Jack, I thought, offering more of a smirk than I intended.

"It's not funny, Jack," she said, actually attempting to parent me. "Mr. Kowicki called. He's your Counselor –"

"I know who he is," I said, biting off the words. *This had better get over with quick, bitch.*

She huffed and held her ground. "He said you missed a lot of school, Jack, and you won't graduate unless you go to summer school –"

"I'm not going to summer school –"

"Jack –"

"I've got a job. That's what I'm going to do, so the hell with Kowicki and school."

She stomped her foot. She actually stomped her foot and put her fists on her hips.

I decided not to hit her yet.

"Jack, I talked to your father today, too, and you haven't been going to work either –"

"There's nothing to do right now." My arms waved around in a slow circle out of my control. "The weather's bad for business right now."

"That's not what he said. You haven't been calling him or checking to see if there's work. Jack, you can't –"

I took three steps toward her and stopped. She dropped her arms and bit her lip. I didn't say anything to her, not a damned thing. I stood and stared down at her and... what, I didn't know... pushed my thoughts directly into her.

"I'm still your mother," she said slowly, pronouncing each word with solid intent.

I yanked her dress up and revealed her gray-haired cunt. "Really?"

She spun away from me and pulled her dress back down. "Jack, this isn't–"

"What? Funny? No, it hasn't been funny in quite some time, has it... what? *Mom,* is that it? *Mom* now, *whore* later when you're sucking my cock?"

"Jackie, don't be mean like that...."

That easy, I thought. She caved that fucking easy. Stupid bitch. I said nothing for a few moments and made her squirm. Then, I said, "School and work is my business now, isn't it? *Mom.*"

She said nothing and stared up at me. Tears filled her eyes so I held her gaze.

"Isn't it, Mom?" I asked straight into her. "School and work is my business now."

"But, Jackie," she said, folding in on herself. "I want you to graduate."

I paused and shot back with, "It's just a lot right now, isn't it? Dad's gone and here we are." Dammit, I thought. "It's just a lot right now."

I knew she struggled with everything, the same as I did, and she crumbled.

I grabbed her and hugged her and thought of us both as pathetic whores. She cried openly in my shoulder and mumbled about her life, my school, my work, Dad, her daughters moving out of state, her family abandoning her after the cancer, on and on and on.

I listened to it all and heard nothing. I held her and rocked her, squeezed her and petted her hair. She looked up and tears poured down her face: Confession bleeding from swollen eyes. Whore to her own son for companionship and lust, she just now realized the consequences of her life.

She kissed me sudden and hard, disconnecting herself from the thought of being my mother. Her authority ended, crushed instantly out of motherhood.

Her daughters from her first marriage had moved to opposite ends of the country, taking her grandchildren away. Her days as a mother in the truest sense were over and she sobbed openly at the realization. Her roles disintegrated around her, leaving her violently empty. No longer a mother, no longer a wife, rarely a grandmother, sister or aunt.

She reduced herself to cook, maid and whore and she hated the perfect fit.

Where did that leave me? I pushed the thought aside and held her in my arms awhile, unable and unwilling to let her go.

A definition failed me, failed us both, and the extreme situation squeezed and crushed in around us, collapsing from every angle. "I'll call Dad tomorrow," I said, brushing her hair back and untangling myself from her.

Her eyes brightened softly and she kissed my cheek. She didn't say anything more and she wiped her face as she walked into the kitchen.

We ate in silence, finding some measure of small talk easier over the last two weeks. But something inside her had changed. Different thoughts coursed through her mind. Something inside her shifted – again – I thought, felt, sensed, somehow, something.

When I fucked her that night she only went through the motions, waiting for me to satisfy myself before rolling over and going to sleep.

I sat up and smoked awhile, watching her back expand and contract with each breath. I listened to her steady rhythm and felt the shift inside myself.

I struggled with fragmented sleep and wondered if Kowicki was right.

Chapter 9

I went to school and paid attention. I went to work and did everything to the best of my ability. I apologized to Dad and told him I'd been having a hard time adjusting to his absence. I went to school and work and did everything I was supposed to do.

I joked around with Dave and Eddie at school and I talked and participated in class. I busted my ass at work and told my dad I loved him and I missed him. I understood in my own way why he'd left and that everything was okay.

Everything.

I was actually anxious to share my day with Mom.

She *was* my mother and I accepted her as she was, regardless of roles and definitions. I felt clear headed and glad to be straight, at least for the time being.

When I got home, my anxiety grew the closer I got the door. Mom had arrived at some conclusion last night and I had no idea what that meant. Argument, peace, sex and sleep, I hadn't seen her since last night.

I told myself I overreacted as I twisted the knob with a shaky hand.

No lights.

I pushed the door the rest of the way open and saw four candles burning on the dining room table. I took a step into the house and saw an unfolded letter next to the candles.

The drama of it all, I thought, nervously stepping up to the table. I peeked into the family room and found empty darkness. I looked past the kitchen and down the hall and saw only a dim, flickering light coming out of the bedroom.

A letter from my dad, I saw immediately, and I didn't touch it – I purposely didn't touch it. I saw it, I didn't touch it and I sat down.

Shit.

And then I read it.

He was sorry. He was pathetic and sorry and he begged her to let him come home. He begged forgiveness for abandoning her. He blamed the cancer for changing their lives, alienating them from the family and destroying their plans for the future.

In a nutshell, he rambled on about being a piece of shit. He would make it up to her, of course, if only she gave him another chance.

I sat embarrassed and ashamed for him, as if I violated a trust of some kind for reading the words of his heart.

Mom enshrined his words and rejected his appeal by the very display. His letter was my salvation and she all but ripped it to shreds. She humiliated him with his own words.

I sat in a chair and absolutely didn't know what to do, or what to expect from her now. She wasn't going to take him back – at least not yet. I looked down the hallway toward her room – her room by invitation only – and I knew my situation had changed completely, regardless of my desire.

For the last time, I considered the door behind me as my one true means of escape. Dave's house, anyone's house, even my dad's apartment: I dismissed them all one by one.

School and work, I told myself. Bury myself in school and work and push through her chaos to the end – to whatever end.

I stood up and found no reason to go to my room. My clothes had taken over Dad's closet and his half of the dresser. She'd rearranged my entire life down to my sock and underwear drawer.

I walked into the bedroom and found her sitting up on the bed. Garter belt, stockings, high heels, sheer nightgown: All in white, all glistening in candlelight, all of it set afire by her red hair and smoldering green eyes.

She smiled and spread her legs as if she couldn't help it. "Jackie," she said in a sultry voice I had not expected. "Did you read his letter?"

I nodded and realized she might not see the subtle movement. "Yes."

"I called him and told him to go to hell today," she said, pulling her legs back together.

Raw sex poured out of her. She didn't seem real. I didn't know... I'd never seen anyone like her in person. The candlelight played off her features, highlighting all the right parts. Her legs looked long and lean in the heels. Her full tits pushed the nightgown into perfect shape.

"I figured as much," I said, unable to take a full step into the room.

"He's a fool," she said. "A pathetic fool. Don't you agree?"

I flexed my fingers and couldn't agree one way or the other. She smoked and leaned her head back against the head board. "We couldn't go on like we were, my sweet Jackie."

I assumed she meant us and I couldn't agree or disagree with that statement either.

She rolled over on her side, curled her legs up and rested her head on her hand. She smiled at me through heavy, dark makeup and retrieved an ashtray from her nightstand. "This is all yours now, Jackie," she said, leaving eye contact for the end.

I didn't quite follow, or didn't want to follow, but I did step into the room and dump the contents of my pockets out on the dresser. I needed motion – some form of action – to arrange my thoughts.

"He pays for everything," she said to my back. "The house, the car, food, clothes... everything."

I stood without anything left to empty from my pockets and forced myself to turn and face her.

She looked good. Scary good. Terrifyingly good.

"—and it's all yours now," she said abruptly. "I want you to have it all."

Mom rolled back over and sat up against the headboard. She reached up, untied her hair and let the flames roll down to her shoulders. "I want you to live in his house, eat his food and drive his car, my beautiful Jackie."

"You do," I said, clearing my voice with the words. I couldn't deny the attraction and my cock raged like iron in my pants.

"—and fuck his woman," she added, grabbing my eyes and releasing. "This is your cunt now, Jackie," she said with alarming ease.

She *had* to say the words – and I struggled to understand my own thoughts but the emphasis was undeniable. She had to say the words, to hear them, to taste them roll off her tongue.

Mom squirmed slightly and I cursed the room's darkness. "You can fuck me anytime you want," she confirmed in case I missed it. She dug her heels in and lifted her hips off the bed. Her hand slid down, opening her legs and letting one finger slip inside.

"Don't be afraid," she said.

Are you kidding, I replied without saying the words.

Mom smiled back and brutally assaulted her cunt without warning.

I flipped on the light switch and blinded us both.

She closed her eyes and viciously attacked herself with both hands.

Her eyes flared open, because, yes, the fucking whore got a little blinded by the sudden fucking light – and was I getting my point across? Was I making it clear to her what the fuck, exactly, was going through my fucking mind?

"You fucking whore," I said in an entirely new way. I slowly removed my clothes and mumbled something about being dirty from work.

She stretched herself open and smiled.

I hated every part of her.

"I'm going to hurt you if you don't stop this shit, Mom," I said, surprised by my shaking voice. I had never been so afraid in my life.

"Then hurt me, Jackie," she said with a cobra's strike.

So I did.

I slapped her face and slammed my cock into her. Her small body shook and she screamed about indecency and lust.

I squeezed her throat and for an instant considered killing her. But then her wicked green eyes flared and she thrust her hips into my attack.

So, I held her in place and fucked her harder.

She cursed me and spat obscenities and vile desires, most of which I did not understand.

I ripped her nightgown off and pulled my cock out of her swollen cunt. *Break.* I released her neck and stood empty and forgotten. *Break.* She curled up on her side and cried openly without restraint. *Break.* I ripped her panties off and spit on her. *Break.*

"You make me sick," someone said and I fell upon her like an animal. I forced my cock into her asshole and slapped the back of her head until she stopped screaming.

"You're a sick, twisted whore," someone said and I dug my fingers into her hip and thigh and controlled her back into my assault. Her soft body collapsed in my hands and I realized the only hard sound in the room: The chaotic click of her heels when they bounced off each other.

"Yes," Mom said softly between tears and curses, but I didn't understand what she meant.

"Pathetic," I replied and I didn't understand what I meant.

Words attacked my body, grinding flesh into emotion and twisting my thoughts into gibberish. I pleased her, I knew, when blood ran from her asshole. I pleased her, I knew, when I muffled her screams with a pillow.

"I love you, Jackie," she said when I allowed her a chance to speak.

Candlelight flickered and I yanked her head back and punched the side of her head.

"I love you," she said again and I yanked the pillow away from her.

I leaned down, opened my mouth and lost my words. I drove a few quick, violent thrusts into her and I couldn't stop shaking. I pushed her face down into the bed and fucked her until she stopped squirming.

Mom looked dead in the waning candlelight, a ghost of someone I once knew. I took a handful of her wet hair and lifted her head off the bed. Her eyes flickered a time or two but she didn't wake up. Slow, uneven breaths escaped her. I dropped her head back to the bed, dismounted and went to piss.

I refused to turn on the bathroom light and avoided the mirror, terrified I would see my own expression and recognize the monster in my eyes. I hadn't done anything, I told myself, and I didn't care what I had done. I accepted the conflict with ease and avoided my gaze as I returned to the bedroom.

I stripped the bed, rolling her from one side to the other, and left her with one pillow and a sheet. She was a pathetic whore and I loved her. She was my mother and a pathetic whore and I loved her and I couldn't cum inside her and I wrapped myself in the comforter and I went to sleep on the couch.

And fuck.

I gave her what she wanted and took what I wanted in return.

Exactly what I wanted.

No. Yes.

No and no and I had done nothing wrong. I didn't understand and I didn't care. She would be different in the morning, I told myself. She would be different and things would be back to normal.

Sleep came fast and caught me unaware.

Chapter 10

I woke to the slightest creak, the barest sound, and I found myself in darkness. Water, then, and awareness slowly returned. Rain, I realized, wrapping myself in the comforter and feeling the sudden pull of sore muscles. The sound of a shower and I knew she was awake.

I lay still and my eyes focused in the gray dawn. I stretched and re-wrapped the comforter. Shadows filled the house and the steady rain relieved my thoughts.

I remembered all of it and felt relieved. I ordered relief if nothing else; I demanded relief. Dad's letter set her off and she would be back to normal.

The shower stopped and saved me from definitions.

My muscles bunched and relaxed as I listened to her dry off and do the things required after a shower.

Mom would be ashamed, of course, I told myself, but all would be right soon enough. She would reconsider Dad's letter and his pathetic attempt at reconciliation. She would see there was no other way.

I wanted a cigarette but not enough move.

The bathroom door opened and she padded softly across the hallway to the bedroom. A contradiction, I told myself, but I didn't know which one of us I meant. A contrast, a battle within: Every definition condemned us both. I ordered my mind to silence and failed.

The gray light brightened and her silence raged in my ears. Quiet as a mouse, her barest breath reduced emotion to dust. *What was she doing? Where was she?* I studied the dining area: the path from the kitchen, the hallway and the bedroom.

The click of high heels surprised me. I scrambled up and into the corner of the couch as she appeared. Mom took one delicate step down into the family room and smiled. I pulled my legs up and tightened the comforter around me.

A sheer white top left her naked from the waist down and the same heels from last night forced an awkward smile.

"You're awake," she said, taking a seat on the couch and resting her hand on my knee. She crossed her legs and smiled like everyone's mother.

"I need a cigarette," I blurted, desperate for time to think. Before I finished the sentence, she stood up.

"I'll get them for you."

I watched her bare ass leave and return in seconds with my cigarettes, lighter and an ashtray. *Maybe not like everyone's mother*, I decided.

Mom resumed her seat, crossed her legs, and let her foot dangle for my pleasure. She lit two cigarettes and handed me one. "Good morning, love," she said again with ease and pleasure in her voice.

"I owe you an explanation," she said before I gathered my thoughts. I sat up in the shadows and saw her face, saw her bruises, the black eye, the swollen cheek. She saw my reaction and pulled her hair aside, revealing last night's destruction.

She smiled and rubbed my leg. "It's good, Jackie," she said, squirming slightly and bouncing her foot. "Don't be ashamed. Don't ever be ashamed with me."

"How is –"

She leaned forward, smoked and put her finger to my lips. She sat back and purposely balanced the ashtray on my leg so we could both reach it.

"I've been waiting for you my entire life, sweetheart," Mom said with overwhelming confidence and control. "And here we are." She scratched the top of her thigh with her fingernail, smoked and stopped swinging her foot.

What the hell was she talking about?

Again she smiled and stopped me from talking. I had nothing to say, anyway. What the hell was there to say?

"You're not a little boy anymore, Jack," she said. "You're the man of the house." She added a pause for effect, then proclaimed: "You're the Master of the house –"

"I'm not the –"

"You *are* the Master –"

"Dad –"

"— isn't here," she said, and I couldn't disagree.

She leaned back, ensuring my view of her exposed crotch. Her curved foot restarted on cue and swung gently in the air. "But you make up your own mind about him," she said and smoked and smiled.

I chased after my thoughts and said nothing.

"You're the man here, now, Jack," she added, chipping away. "You didn't run away like a coward. You didn't leave me when I needed you." She crushed out her cigarette and put both hands on my leg. "Everything around you is yours now, Jack. Including me."

I replied without words. She saw my discomfort and smiled softly. "Let me get you something, love." She stood in full display and smiled down at me. "What would you like?"

I stared from her bare cunt up to her bruised face and found no answers.

"Anything, love," she said, focusing my unstable attention.

"Orange juice," I said, shaking my head. "Coke."

She smiled and turned to fetch.

Like a dog.

Like a bitch.

Like a machine.

She needed help. Serious help. Professional help. One of us did, anyway.

I listened to her pour the Coke, add some ice, then disappear from the kitchen. She returned with my glass and the tube of KY.

She handed me both and disrupted my timing. "You saved me, my beautiful Jack," she said, snatching a quick pause. "You have no idea how you saved me."

"Mom, what are you talking about?"

"I love you so much, my beautiful sweetheart. You have no idea."

"Mom I –"

"Everything I have is yours now. Everything your father has is yours. But I don't think you understand what I'm saying."

I nodded and found no words. *Who was she now,* I wondered. *And who was I?*

I took a deep breath and crushed out my cigarette. Coke bubbled in my mouth, I swallowed and said nothing. I wanted her to talk, to expel whatever haunted her. I thought of calling Dad, but for what? He'd played his cards and left the table empty handed.

Mom touched her bruises and smiled. "You have so much beauty inside you, Jackie."

"Beauty. Yes," I replied. Of course.

"You have so much strength."

"Strength."

"You'll beat me more," She said and I knew she was right.

"My protector," she said when I didn't reply. "My savior."

She didn't make sense. None of it made sense.

"Beautiful," she said, as if answering my unspoken question. "Last night was beautiful with you, my Jackie. Your power, your strength. You were a man with me last night – the most beautiful man I've ever been with."

None of it registered, yet her words felt like some sick, twisted truth. I squeezed my hard cock between my thighs and she smiled.

"I am your whore now," she continued when I said nothing. "Your cook, your maid, anything you want me to be."

"Anything but my mother," I snapped, hearing my voice from a distance.

"If you'd like, I can be that, too," she replied without missing a beat.

"If I'd like." I spit the words at her. *What the fucking hell?*

"Is that what you want me to be? Your mother?" She gently slid the comforter down to my waist and let her long fingernails barely scrape my skin. She found my cock and softly stroked, curling around herself and smiling at me.

I couldn't see anything in the deep gray, rainy morning. Washed out colors revealed nothing and reduced everything to the unfamiliar.

"Do you want to talk more?" she asked. "Or do you want me to suck your cock now?"

Despite my fear or because of it, my cock grew strong and hard in her hand. I said nothing and hated myself.

"You didn't cum last night," she said, pulling the comforter down and exposing me. "I know you're very confused right now and this isn't helping."

Which didn't stop her, of course. But, she wasn't here to help me, I told myself, and I didn't understand my own heart.

She leaned down, kissed and licked me, and held my eyes for approval.

I ran my hand through her fading red hair and watched her engulf me. Within seconds, I squeezed her head, thrust twice into her and filled her mouth with cum.

She gulped and swallowed, licked and cleaned me, and returned the comforter to its original position. She delicately wiped her lips with one finger and smiled. "So much," she said, as if to herself.

She reached for my cigarettes and told me I was beautiful.

I didn't know what to say, think or feel. I accepted the lit cigarette from her and felt dead inside. I felt dead and more alive than I'd ever felt before and I hated every bit of her – and loved her, and felt sickened by the thought of her.

And everything.

And nothing.

"I know you're confused right now, love," she said, and I wanted to kill her. She rested her chin on my upright knee and offered a genuine, loving smile. "This must be overwhelming. I made the bed if you want to get some sleep. I imagine you didn't sleep very well out here last night."

"Bitch," I said, wishing I'd said nothing.

"*Your* bitch," she corrected, unfolding herself and standing up. "Is this okay?" she asked suddenly, displaying herself for me. "Am I sexy for you, Jackie? I want to be sexy for you. Is that okay?"

I reached up and gently rubbed her dry cunt. "You're sexy," I admitted.

But she wasn't my mother anymore. Not even close. She wasn't anything of the person who raised me – yet she was precisely my mother, and I didn't understand any of it. I rubbed her dry clit and didn't give a shit about either one of us.

I couldn't take it anymore. I couldn't fight it, or roll with it, or struggle with it, or examine it, or make sense of it. I didn't give a shit anymore.

All I had to do was survive.

I swung my feet around and set them on the floor. The comforter slid off of its own accord, leaving me naked in front of her. I squirted too much KY on my fingers and smacked her cunt without warning, easily opening her and creating a large, slick mess.

She stepped apart and swayed to whatever mysterious rhythm drove her. I saw the bruises inside both thighs and knew she was right: I wasn't finished hurting her.

But not now, something told me. Not yet.

I sat back on the couch and let her mount me, let her thrust and work to please me. She rolled her hips over me, leaned down and kissed my neck. "Thank you, sweetheart," she said to someone.

"Cum," I told her and she did, quietly without fanfare and trumpets.

I mentioned something about sleep and she followed me down the hallway.

"Don't ever stop fucking me," she said, tucking me in tight and kissing my forehead.

I didn't reply and knew nothing lasted forever.

"Go to sleep, my beautiful boy," she said, casting a spell upon me. "I'll be here when you wake up."

And she was, sitting right there on the edge of the bed as if she'd never moved.

Outside, thunder arrived, and the afternoon looked little different from the morning.

Chapter 11

At first I didn't understand anything inside or out. I had drifted through the last two months, participating in everything like a movie extra.

Work picked up as the weather changed and I welcomed the long hours, although discussions with my dad had long since deteriorated into nothing more than mumblings about the day's labor.

I'd told Kowicki the Counselor on the last day of class I wasn't going to summer school, or any school for that matter; that I was done, finished with it, with everything. Just too much. Too much in my brain.

Dad was desperate to come home, which I didn't understand, especially after listening to his phone conversations with his whore-slash-wife.

And she was, I decided, his wife and my whore. I used her for food and shelter. I used her for sex. I used her for a punching bag.

The house was clean and the food was good. I paid no rent, no bills, no anything. I wasn't particularly happy or sad but I didn't give a shit one way or the other.

Mom was a difficult bitch to understand. I told her how livid Dad got when I told him I'd quit school. She laughed and said he would never understand.

She used him for money and she used his money on me. She wrapped him in guilt and dangled him like a carrot in front of me. I denied the similarities and told myself I got the better deal.

"No, Jimmy," she said to him on a beautiful summer morning. Mom pressed her pelvis against the kitchen counter and stared blankly through the window. Her eyes burned into the farmer's field outside with such cruelty, such devastation, I almost felt sorry for Dad.

I slid a finger into Mom's cunt and gently rolled her hips back and forth. She switched hands with the phone and used my shoulder for balance. Up on her toes, feet spread, she gave me a quick smile and returned to the phone.

"I want a new car, Jimmy," she said with disdain and authority. "And I want Jack to pick it out. What's difficult about that?" She tilted the phone away from her ear so I could hear Dad.

"You want me to buy him a car," he protested, but the underlying tone of his voice said he'd already lost.

"No," she said as if correcting a child. "I want *him* to pick it out. It's *my* car."

Dad snorted and didn't reply.

Mom smiled and pushed my fingers deep into her cunt. Her olive eyes glazed over. She held the phone away from her mouth, gasped and released, and returned to the phone with ease.

"... and you're going to drive me broke," he was saying.

"You did this to yourself," she snapped and lit into him. "You left us, remember? How's your whore doing?" She pressed the phone to her leg for a few seconds as if she didn't want to hear the answer.

"... is bullshit, Jane," he said on return, careful to even out his tone. He'd learned the tone of his voice cost him money. "You won't see me, or even talk to me unless you want something."

Mom cupped the mouth piece and pointed at it. "He's learning," she whispered at me with a smile. She freed the phone, cupped and released my balls and turned her fire on him.

"See you for what?" she asked pointedly, biting off and spitting her questions at him. "To talk about what? Coming home? You want to come home now? For what? You love me now, is that it? You love me again –"

"Jane –"

"Did your whore leave you? Is that it?"

"Jane," he tried again. "I made a mistake."

I slid three fingers into her cunt and my thumb in her asshole. I lifted her up and massaged everything together. She staggered and held the phone away from herself, stealing breaths and panting.

"I'm sorry," Dad begged, carrying the conversation, but sounding small and insignificant through the phone.

I stretched her wide in every direction and bent her over the counter.

"I still love you," Dad said with static-filled sadness.

Mom gasped at the phone and thrust her hips back into my touch.

"I've always loved you," he said.

I abruptly released her, adjusted her body and pressed her face down on the counter. She hissed like a cat and spread her feet further apart.

"... are you still there? ... Jane...?"

I slid most of my other hand into her asshole and whispered in her ear, "Answer him."

Her body vibrated and tears filled her eyes. She slowly brought the phone to her mouth. "I'm here," she said, unable to steady her voice. "I'm listening."

He misunderstood her shaking voice, of course. But then, he actually thought he wanted her back. He only wanted and end to his guilt, I realized, to tell himself he repaired the damage and put everything behind him.

I curved my hand into a point and thrust completely into her.

Her head lolled forward and back. I studied her profile and watched her breath escape in short, tight bursts. Her eyes rolled back in her head and I couldn't tell if she'd had an orgasm or not.

My hand disappeared into and reemerged from her ass in a blurry, twisted nightmare. I lost myself into her, into Mom, and reemerged from a hell I couldn't remember.

She arched her back, lifted her ass up and rocked back into my attack.

Dad couldn't move on, and I couldn't get him out of my head. I stared at the telephone and waited for answers.

Mom cried under my assault and offered it as a lie to Dad. "Where did it all go, Jimmy?" she asked in a broken voice held together by tears. "Did you love me when you walked out the door?"

I pulled my hand out of her asshole, unzipped myself and shoved my cock into her without thought or concern.

Her mouth opened in a silent scream. She dragged the phone back across the counter and cupped the mouthpiece in her hands. I held her neck to the counter while her body erupted in rapid convulsions.

She brought the phone within earshot and we heard, "... for each other. You know that. I did a horrible thing. Please don't let it wreck our lives –" Again, she muffled him with her hands over the receiver.

I fucked her and... and, what? Listened to Dad whine? Listened to Mom force him to buy me a car? Listened to the sound of our bodies crashing together? Listened to the sound of my mind falling apart?

I pulled out, slammed back in and drove her against the counter with hard, rapid thrusts. I slowed enough to let her catch her breath and speak.

"You make it all sound so easy, Jimmy. You make it all sound as if it's up to me." Her breathing matched my short, hard thrusts, but her eyes focused laser sharp. "Why am I supposed to believe you? How are you going to show me the truth?"

Truth, I thought.

And I heard his tears. And I understood why he wasn't here. He quietly cried and said, "I'll do anything," while I fucked his wife in the ass.

Mom snorted and I tightened my hand around the back of her neck. I stood her back up and continued my assault. She brought the phone up and tightly laughed. "*Anything* doesn't mean anything to me, Jimmy. Not anymore. I'm not the same woman you abandoned –"

I felt the word cut him.

" – I want a man who knows who he is, and knows what he wants to do for me."

She dropped the phone to her thigh and braced herself.

I attacked her with a short burst of violence. "Say when," I offered.

"When," she accepted. She brought the phone back to her mouth. "What do you want to do for me, Jimmy?"

Silence.

She hissed, I squeezed, and again she pressed the phone to her thigh.

I fucked her slow and pictured him at work, behind his desk or pacing like an anxious, angry prisoner.

Mom brought the phone up and asked, "Well?" with little interest in the answer.

Dad sighed and finally asked, "What kind of car does he want?"

She scoffed and rubbed the side of my face, licking me as if she were an animal. We locked eyes and she brought the phone up. "It's always money, isn't it, Jimmy? You want to buy your way out of everything."

I stopped abruptly and left my cock buried in her asshole. She tried to squirm but my hand on the back of her neck locked her in place. I heard Dad talking but she held the phone at arm's length so we couldn't make out his words.

She unclenched her muscles and sagged on the counter, completely subdued and relaxed. I rubbed the small of her back and slowly fucked her, feeling every soft, wet inch of her.

She slid the phone back to her mouth. In a dreamy, absent voice, she asked, "What, Jimmy? What are you saying? You want to buy me more stuff? Buy your way back into my bed?"

"No," he mumbled. "I don't know what you want. What do you want?"

I yanked her up by her hair, cutting off her response to him. "Filthy whore," I whispered. I took her hand with the phone and brought it up to her mouth. "Say goodbye."

"Buy me the car, Jimmy," she said without emotion. "Since that's all you know how to do."

She held the button down, killing the call; then she released the phone and let the cord's tension pull it off the counter and bounce it across the floor.

I grunted like an animal, shook and shuddered and filled her ass with cum.

Mom moaned and squirmed as I flooded into her.

I released her and she turned and collapsed into my arms. "You take such good care of me," she said, or something similar, and our embrace fit perfectly in place.

The odd, alternating squawk of the abandoned phone filled the kitchen. Mom smiled to herself and retrieved the phone, hanging it back on the wall. "I love you, sweetheart," she said with her back to me. Then, turning toward me, she asked as if she'd forgotten the answer, "You know that, don't you?"

I ignored the question to hurt her.

Her damp, nasty eyes radiated anything but love. "Let's have Daddy buy you a car," she said, moving toward me in a slow motion attack. She spit out the words, then released me. "Let me take a shower and we'll go car shopping."

"Nasty whore," I said, referring mostly to myself.

Chapter 12

The car changed everything. Maybe it was more like the car signaled a transition... somewhere. I didn't know. Things changed – the *feel* of it – or things progressed, or declined, depending on how I looked at it. A small shift here, a small change there, the slightest bump in the night and all hell broke loose in slow motion. Anyway, I put it all down to the car: the beginning of the end.

But nothing really ended, either. Nothing ever does.

So, fuck. Me.

Mom forcing Dad to buy me a car while I fucked her sounded more amusing than it turned out. A lot of things about her sounded more amusing than they turned out. I wasn't getting ahead of myself, but I knew she was a rough ride from the moment she first begged me to stay.

In public, she dressed like a mom; a well-dressed mom, but a mom nonetheless.

She embraced early summer in white heels, purse and a bow in her auburn hair. Flower print dress down to her knees, she crossed her legs at the *Pontiac* dealer and seemed mildly bored. She also found the reality of forcing someone to buy a car less than amusing, albeit, I expected, for different reasons than my own.

I told Bob the car salesman I was – that my *mother* was – willing to wait for a black Trans Am, and, yes, the red one was quite nice, but come on. Really?

Bob agreed, of course, in spirit, but a photo on the wall behind him suggested his seven children, three dogs, and one frowning wife all found red the perfect color.

Mom strummed her fingernails on her purse and drew my attention. She smiled at all the right times, I thought. She acted, reacted and behaved superbly. She perked up when it came time to call Dad and I watched her share a smile with Bob.

A grand performance, indeed.

I stood up and paced the showroom. Embarrassment caught me unaware and I didn't want to hear any part of the conversation. I read the Service Policy sign four times while my dad paid for a car over the telephone that I could not begin to afford in person. The insurance alone was a stretch.

Seventeen year old boys and sports cars were not meant for each other.

I saw my father's exhaustion on Bob's face and heard it in his voice. I blinked and the salesman reviewed a document with Mom for her signature. I blinked again and wished I'd disappeared.

My freshly fucked mom sat like she owned the world, keeping her legs crossed and her dress just above the knee. She signed everything Bob slid in front of her and cast me a sidelong wink when he looked in his desk for a moment.

She looked amused and bored at the same time, anxious for the deal to be done, anxious for something always out of her reach. Maybe I just read myself into her.

I'd grown accustomed to my ever-present stomach ache over the last couple weeks. The car would arrive in a few days and a sharp pain in my gut struck me when I moved to shake Bob's hand.

"You're a lucky kid," he said, trained to keep his tone even and meaningful.

I felt like a whore, which was something I doubted he'd expect me to say.

"I want to buy lunch," Mom said afterward, as she swung her legs up into her car. I closed the door without answering and walked around to the driver's side.

Wasn't the car enough, I thought. Where did it end?

I reminded myself that nothing ever ended, smiled at her and said nothing.

She twisted and put her arm on mine. "Jack, let's go to that little place in the A&P parking lot." She fumbled in her purse for her sunglasses.

I looked down, saw the KY and started the engine. I headed toward lunch on the other side town and wallowed in silence. My stomach wanted anything but food. Guilt, embarrassment, fear, lust and entitlement all brewed a shitty cup of coffee and left me nauseous.

"You deserve the car," she said, adjusting the large rimmed glasses and looking straight ahead. "Where would I be without you?"

Alone, I knew. Her sisters barely called her once a week. Her daughters called her once a month. We drove the remaining few minutes in silence.

I pulled into the *A&P* parking lot but stopped short of *The Griddle Restaurant*. I swung the car around and parked in a space between the two buildings as if I could not decide between the two establishments.

"Open your purse," I said without emotion either way. My stomachache fought my headache and I wanted something to hit.

Mom obeyed without a word and didn't understand yet.

I reached into her purse without invitation and pulled out the tube of KY. "Take off your panties," I said with equal lack of enthusiasm.

She understood now. "Jack," she replied and hesitated. "It's broad daylight."

"Pull up your dress," I said, ignoring her.

Mom complied to the tone of my voice, I thought, and my fingers slid into her, wetting, working and opening her to position. She removed her sunglasses and set them on the dashboard, spread her legs and held on to the car door.

"Jackie, please...," she offered in weak protest. She worked her hips in a tight circle, pulled her dress up to her waist and pushed my fingers deep inside. "Please, Jack.... People will see...."

I leaned over, rocked her back and tilted her seat.

"Someone we know might see us." She gasped and braced herself on my shoulder and the car door.

I unbuckled my pants and maneuvered in front of her. She guided me inside and I fucked her like a whore in broad daylight. Her breath escaped in short bursts next to my ear. Her hand tightened on my shoulder and her legs bounced off the car interior.

I looked out the back window of the car and used her like an animal. Mild, early afternoon traffic rolled by, shoppers in the distance walked to and from the grocery store and only one car drove close enough where they *may* have seen what we were about.

I fucked her and couldn't have cared less about her or the world around her. "I'm going to cum," I declared as if reading a report.

"Yes," she replied between grunts.

I pushed her head back and saw a frightened and ashamed woman. Her eyes filled with green tears and her hair and makeup rested on the verge of destruction.

I pushed back on the seat and slammed my cock into her several more times. She winced and released several muffled cries. Her fingernails dug into my shoulder and I exploded into her.

I pulled out and pushed off, rolling myself back to the driver's seat. I buckled up and reached for my cigarettes.

Mom caught her breath and reached down for her panties.

"No," I told her, lighting two cigarettes and handing her one. "Leave them there. You should never have worn them in the first place."

"But, Jack –"

"No," I softly insisted, pushing her thigh so she couldn't close her legs or lower her dress. I pinched her cunt and watched my sperm ooze out of her.

"My dress, Jack," she whispered, beginning to cry. "It's going to stain, to leave a mark. Oh, Jack...." She squirmed and quickly wiped her eyes as I kept pressure on her dripping cunt.

"Just relax a minute and have your cigarette." I pinched and toyed with her as if she were a machine. I smoked and considered her as a new toy, or a specimen ripe for experimentation.

She cried quietly and her hand shook when she tried to smoke – which made her cry more. Her thighs vibrated as she struggled to hold her position.

"Please, Jack," she begged.

I released her and pointed at her panties. "Wipe yourself, then give them to me."

She obeyed with her cigarette dangling out of her mouth. "Oh, my God," she whispered. "Oh, my God, Jack."

She handed me her panties and I dropped them out my window.

Mom looked shocked but said nothing. She wiggled and pulled her dress back down and fumbled in her purse for makeup.

I started the car and idled over to the restaurant. "Buy me lunch," I said, as I parked and turned off the engine.

She didn't reply.

I understood and waited while she repaired her face and hair. She snapped her purse closed and glanced nervously at me, again fixing her eyes out the front window. "I won't wear them anymore," she said quietly.

"Never," I agreed, then considered.

"At least ask first," I decided, and she seemed to accept the rule.

I couldn't tell what garbled mess ran through her mind, but I watched her compose herself and told myself I was lucky. A quiet and tentative, "I love you, Jack," only added to my bewilderment of her nature.

"I love you, too," I said without surprise. A whore, cook, maid and meal ticket all rolled into my mother: What was there not to love?

I hated myself for a moment as I got out of the car and went around to open her door. She got out and spun for me with a hesitant look in her eye.

"No stains," I said without paying attention, closing the car door behind her.

"You didn't look," she replied, petulant enough for action.

I took her arm in mine and led her to the restaurant. *Dog on a chain*, I thought, feigning concern. *Bitch on a leash*.

She chain-smoked and hid behind her menu. Her hands didn't shake enough for anyone to notice, but I didn't want her to break down in the restaurant. I told her, "Dad says I should take a week's vacation soon. I thought we could go somewhere and pay for it with his credit card."

Anything to hit him with, I thought, and turn her attention outward. Her hands stopped shaking, she closed the menu and smiled.

I swore one of her razor green eyes twitched.

I smiled at the waitress and ordered something mundane. Mom followed suit and we blew cigarette smoke at each other across the table.

"We'll go somewhere in your new car," she offered, blending in as much sadistic humor as possible. She played with the salt shaker and the other stuff on the table as if it were a puzzle.

I nodded and said nothing. We seldom went out in public together: The grocery store, miscellaneous shopping, or I'd drop her off at her hair appointments. We seldom went anywhere that forced us to confront each other directly – like restaurants.

I toyed with my cigarette in the ashtray and studied my discomfort. I'd just fucked her in the parking lot. I had just fucked my mother in the parking lot and now we're on a lunch date – after forcing my dad to buy me a car I didn't need. I pictured her crumpled panties in the middle of the parking lot, smiled, drew smoke and exhaled.

She was my mother.

Mom.

A fading thought and a lovely memory, but only her reflection stared back at me from across the table. A dream within a nightmare, or some shit. She gave birth to me and for a time assumed the motherly role; but here now, across from me, sat a whore who sought only vengeance against the man who left her.

I was reminded of my dad being her third husband.

What did all this make me? I thought of her across from me now, without panties – without everything else that went along with her panties – and I said, "We could go north," as if words could save me.

She sipped her coffee and readily smiled. "Yes. It's beautiful up there."

I couldn't read her tone or match her words to her expression. I realized how little attention I actually paid to her inflections, at least to the point where it truly mattered. I controlled her with sex.

We controlled each other with sex.

By her design, I thought, as the food arrived. The phrase rang true. I felt reconstructed, or under construction.

Mom ran on pure complication and diversion and never held a straight line for long. She was an actress in the role of a lifetime, playing opposite her own son. I wondered if the game had gotten away from her. Or was everything going precisely to some twisted script wrapped around her brain? Was I over-thinking the sordid mess or was there something else in it for her besides lust and vengeance?

What inner demons drove her soul?

I frowned inwardly and wondered what inner demons drove my own soul.

I needed a joint.

Our silent confrontation raged in my head. I finished the bland sandwich and shoved the plate away. Sitting with her in the restaurant left me with no escape, no way out, nothing except forced, almost ritualistic, self examination.

I really needed a joint – and some time away from her – already regretting the offer of a vacation together.

Mom declined the waitress's offer of a carry out box. She'd barely eaten anything. She hadn't planned on leaving her panties in the parking lot the first time I used her in public.

I watched the wheels spin in her head. I *felt* the wheels spin in her head and I couldn't decide who invaded whom. I thought again of her as an actress with a script of her own design and reminded myself nothing really ended and nothing really mattered.

I lit a cigarette and watched her accept the check. The waitress didn't hesitate. Mom looked every bit the middle aged mother out to lunch with her son. She unsnapped her purse and laid out a precise tip. She sipped her water and finally looked at me for direction.

I smoked and considered fucking her again when we got back to the car. She squirmed in her seat as if reading my mind and was not, I saw, entirely pleased with me. Hers was a personal game she played in private with select players, no doubt with a select result in mind— and I wondered at that moment how many people had sat in my seat before me.

As I opened the car door for her, I felt drowned and done, in way over my head at best. I told her I was going out for a while, and I'd be dropping her off at home. She relaxed and told me I didn't have to spend every minute with her.

"Don't lose your friends," she said in a tone I couldn't place. She didn't wait for me to open the door for her, turned back and smiled. "You go have fun, Jack. I'll be here when you get home."

The finality of her words bothered me the rest of the night. I stretched and flexed like a rubber band, never able to leave her completely behind, even for one night.

She sighed from somewhere and studied me a moment – a quick moment she caught and released. She drifted in and out of roles, I told myself and found my headache too intense for analytical observation.

I rubbed her thigh and pushed my thumb against her bare mound. "You shaved yourself," I said, surprised by the look. I'd never seen anything like it. My cock stretched out ready for action, but my headache slapped it back down.

"Is it okay?" she asked, looking down at herself. "It's easier than trimming."

What a fucked up conversation to have with one's mother, I thought. "It's fine," I told her. "I like it."

She visibly relaxed and reached for my cigarettes. "I was out this morning and bought a carpet shampooer."

I didn't make the connection.

Mom shrugged and crossed between amusement and embarrassment. "The couch would've been ruined if I didn't clean it." Her tentative words begged further expression.

I remembered pissing on her and said nothing, completely at a loss for words.

"I love you so much, sweetheart," she said, saving the moment and running her hand through my dirty hair. "Are you happy here? With me? Do I make you happy?"

The string of soft questions swirled my thoughts into cerebral goop.

"I want to please you," she said, relentless in her gentle attack. "I want to please you so much it hurts sometimes."

Mom, Jane, bitch, whore, I named her nothing and thought her reaction strange for someone who'd been pissed on the night before. "Have you been to sleep?" I asked with a quick shift, realizing she'd been up when I got home and had since been shopping.

"Not really," she answered and I saw the exhaustion around her eyes, her amplified wrinkles and the tight sag of her shoulders. "I love you, Jack," she said, obviously needing me to reply.

"I love you, too," I said.

She smiled as if she didn't believe me. "Promise me you'll never hold anything back," she said with sudden intensity. "You can do anything you want to me. I love everything you do to me. Please remember that, sweetheart."

Her pale green eyes flashed yellow and she looked away, out the window, and smoked nervously.

"What about pissing on you?" I asked bluntly.

Nothing at first, then she turned and offered a faint smile. "Anything," she confirmed. "Pleasing you pleases me." After a slight pause, she added, "I'll never say 'no' to you, Jack."

The odd conversation sat well with my hangover. I nursed the Coke and waited for her to continue.

And she did. Mom had much to say. Words boiled up inside her. I marveled at the effort she put into expression, as if she had to say certain things in certain ways.

"I want you to explore yourself," she said. "With me. Use me, Jack, anyway you want."

My hard-on won out over my headache.

"There is an animal in you, Jack," she continued. "An animal in all of us."

She straightened up on the bed as if she'd surprised herself. She took a breath, offered a slight smile and quickly kissed my forehead. "I just want you to know I'm here for you."

Mom stood up before I could answer. I rubbed her belly and the top of her mound, and she smiled. "Can I bring you breakfast?"

"You should sleep," I offered, releasing her and stretching out.

"After breakfast," she replied, leaving me drenched in afternoon sunlight.

In what felt like seconds, she returned with eggs, bacon, orange juice, toast and coffee and set the tray on the dresser.

In seconds.

My interest in the missing time fell away when she briefly knelt on the bed, pulled my blanket down and exposed my cock. She set the tray before me, kissed me on the cheek and crawled on top of me.

Mom sucked my cock while I ate. She stroked and rubbed, looked up, smiled and consumed me. "Is this okay?" she asked, waiting for my obvious answer.

"Yes," I replied, scratching her head like a dog.

She smiled and resumed her efforts, once again the perfect whore.

I finished eating, set the tray aside and ejaculated in her mouth.

She gulped and smiled and came up licking her lips. She wiped her mouth, careful of her fingernails, and knelt in front of me on the edge of the bed.

"I need sleep," she said, as if waiting for my permission.

I unfolded myself out of bed and offered her the space.

"Thank you," she said dreamily, pulling off her shoes and top and climbing into bed. "For everything," she added as an afterthought. "For staying here with me, for loving me."

I said nothing and walked naked to the bathroom.

"You're so good to me," I heard her say as she slowly drifted to sleep.

The animal inside, I thought, finding myself with an empty afternoon. A flood of emotion overran my thoughts. My body responded with pain deep inside my stomach, like an ever-present fist punching me from the inside out.

I showered and paced the house in a quiet rage against both my physical pain and the self-generated, emotional cage surrounding me. She hadn't done this, I reminded myself, tasting every vile, acidic thought. I couldn't even define what this was, let alone fabricate excuses.

I felt like a human experiment, although the rationale for the sensation evaded me. I returned to the familiarity of everything: the entire thing – the thing with her. I felt created, assembled and manipulated and again the rationale escaped me.

Fine, she was my mother, but I was not a child, not really. I stood in the gray space, the transitional space, between childhood and adulthood. At seventeen years old, I told myself I possessed enough mental and emotional wherewithal to understand and appreciate my actions and reactions. But I couldn't help feeling I'd missed something vital in my transaction with Mom.

I lacked some unknown ingredient, for lack of a better term; like a part of me was missing – or, no – like a part of me was left behind, as if I'd left a part of myself behind.

I had abandoned myself.

Somewhere back *there*.

I sounded crazy, panicked for a moment and found myself standing in the garage. I sat on the garden tractor and regretted having no lawn to mow. I looked from her car to my old motorcycle, to the endless assortment of garden tools and gadgets. The scent of gasoline, motor oil, fertilizer and dust scratched the inside of my nose and throat.

I didn't move to air the place out. Something felt wrong – beyond fucking my own mother and the absolute turn on of it. Something felt disjointed and out of place and I was terrified of discovering my missing ingredient.

I hated the thought of learning more things; acquiring more information. I hated myself more than her and so I was stuck. She was damaged, broken in a way I would never understand – in a way she probably didn't understand. From the day she'd sucked my dick and begged me to stay I knew something was wrong with her.

And in that same instant I realized something was wrong with me.

I loved fucking her. I loved knowing she was crazy and knowing she was my mother. I loved watching her face when I fucked her. I fucked her *because* she was my mother. She was a fifty-seven year old woman and I couldn't keep my cock out of her.

What the hell was the matter with me? I wanted to go fuck her again, right then. I convinced myself she needed sleep and rest. She needed energy so I could fuck her some more.

So I could piss on her.

My cock hardened like iron and I paced the garage like an animal.

There is an animal in you, she'd said.

I hated the bright, sunlit day. I craved gray sky, rain and storms. I blinked and found myself in the basement – again pacing, again denying light – moving slowly while my eyes adjusted.

What the fuck, what the fuck, what the fuck?

I had to stop this shit, somehow – end it. I laughed inwardly at the thought. How would it end? How could it end?

Again, I held a laugh.

How could it *not* end badly?

I slumped down against the concrete wall and couldn't stop shaking. The cold, damp basement curled around my thoughts and left me anything but comfortable. I reveled in it, of course: in the misery, the drama, the arcane insanity of it all.

Cold sweat soaked my clothes, and I sensed the fight of a lifetime upon me.

I felt like a fucking animal and I hated her for recognizing me.

I focused around the basement, concentrating on the space, sorting and analyzing every box, every discarded item unable to be thrown out, given away, or simply freed from bondage. A few boxes held Dad's things he had not taken with him.

I remembered the bitch packing them up and me carrying them down here for her. Small things, stupid things, some things she had given him and some things he had simply forgot to pack.

Cruelty entered my thoughts and an anxious need for strong survival, for dominating my surroundings, for protecting my place, my situation, my territory.

She wanted the animal. Stupid bitch. She wanted me to release everything and anything. She wanted primal instinct.

What was my primal instinct?

Not to run. Not to cower in the basement like a beaten dog. Not to cry like a child afraid of his own shadow.

I pushed myself up and squatted low, feeling every muscle burn inside my body. My fingers flexed and released. Raw energy and adrenaline raced through my veins.

She had no idea what she asked for, I told myself, standing and stretching and heading toward the stairs.

I stood over her sleeping body and stripped off my clothes. She snored lightly, deep in sleep. I stroked my cock and looked down at her. She could sleep later, I thought, pulling back the covers and exposing her naked body.

She slowly opened her eyes and turned toward me. She stretched and considered me without expression. "What took you so long?" she asked quietly, stretching again and offering a mild smile.

Her deep eyes shifted and darkened like the sea when she finally looked into my eyes.

I returned her smile and gave her what she asked for.

Chapter 14

She moaned painfully, rolled over and watched me dress for work. "Where you going?" she mumbled in a thick voice. Then, "Oh," when she saw my work uniform.

"It must be morning," she said, wincing, stretching and taking a deep breath. She laid her head back down when I didn't reply.

I'd beaten her, fucked her, pissed on her and abused her last night, but the details escaped me. I felt as if I was recovering from a drunken rage, except I didn't drink anything last night. I didn't even smoke a joint.

I stood over her, straight as an arrow, and buttoned my pants. She smiled up at me as if she herself were recovering from a binge. And, I supposed, we both were.

I grabbed a handful of her filthy hair and lifted her head up off the pillow. I kissed her hard, shoving my tongue in her mouth. She responded willingly, kissing me with her entire squirming body. She purred like a kitten when I let her go.

"You taste like shit," I said.

"I'm sorry," she replied.

Mom pushed and kicked the sheets down with obvious, uncoordinated effort. "Fuck me before you go?" she asked absently, still half asleep. She rubbed her red thighs and patted around the bed until she found the KY.

"No," I said, cutting off the word and sliding my belt through my pant loops.

She lay back and released a sigh, unsure if my answer was good or bad. Her arm stretched out and dropped uselessly to the bed. Then, as if an afterthought: "Want me to suck your cock before you go?"

"No, you stupid bitch," I said. "Enough." I walked over to the dresser and gathered my wallet, keys, pen, pencil and pocket screwdriver. Her body shifted in the mirror and distorted my view.

Mom sprawled out naked, drifting in and out of sleep. She struggled admirably to stay awake while I was there. "What do you want for dinner?" she asked, again squirming around and wincing from the effort.

"Anything you want," I replied without interest. I debated fucking her again, driving her hard for a quick finish and go to work. Instead, I said, "We're going to pick up the car tonight," and left it flat between us.

"Hmm-mm," she sighed, rolling over and waking up a bit. "Are you going to fuck me in the back seat?" She smiled like a child and toyed with her finger on the soiled sheets.

"Wash the bedding," I told her, ignoring her question. I left the room before she could respond. "I'll be home late," I called out to her, wasting no energy on my way out of the house.

I sat in my car and forgot to breath. I couldn't decide who won – or when, exactly, I decided I was at war with her.

I claimed her like a prize last night and used her for purely aggressive release. Humiliation, degradation – damnit, I wished I could remember the specifics. I refused to stop even after she passed out: I remembered that. I pissed on her face and fucked her some more. I couldn't remember.

Fuck that shit, anyway. And fuck her, too.

She thanked me last night and asked for more this morning.

I was losing my fucking mind, right in the middle, half in, half out.

Love and war, I thought, starting the car and driving to work. I missed everything good about the journey. Maybe I didn't understand something, or I misunderstood something. Maybe I didn't know what she meant by *animal*.

Maybe I was just as afraid of her as I had been the first time....

A sinking feeling, or sunk, or lost, I shook my head as if I answered myself. The first time, what? What first time was I talking about? Not Dad leaving; not that, but... what?

I mixed empty words and smelled the city forty-five minutes into my drive. What was Dad's state of mind, I wondered. What would he think when I showed up in a new car tomorrow?

I laughed and called him assorted names, none more flattering than loser asshole. If I could figure out a way to ensure my mother's hole forever, I'd quit working for him and spend my days fucking his wife.

She was too old, though, I thought with a laugh. I couldn't imagine fucking her when she was eighty. I'd let her suck my cock, and somehow I knew it would be enough for her. I laughed again, thinking of the toothless old hag slurping on my cock with cum dribbling down her wrinkled neck.

Too bad she wasn't twenty years younger.

I pulled into the parking lot at work and knew I was five minutes late.

Fuck him, I thought. *Loser asshole.*

Raw energy raced through my body and I put it all down to Mom. She prompted last night's outburst that left her exhausted this morning. She bit off exactly enough to chew.

Thank you, bitch, I thought, as I walked up to Don the Lead Installer. One sniff confirmed the drunken maniac reeked of booze and bar tramps.

"Yo, Don," I said, walking up to the skinny bastard. "What's up?"

"You're late," he said, avoiding my eyes. He took a quick glance and smiled. "Finish loading the truck. The stuff's inside the door." He turned and disappeared into the shop, up to the front, for whatever the hell reason.

I huffed and puffed and loaded the old van up. I climbed in the passenger side, grateful Don liked to drive, and considered my chances with a drunken furnace installer on the open road.

Fuck the world, I thought, lighting a cigarette and putting my foot up on the dirty dashboard.

Eleven hours later, I relished the evening exhaustion. I hadn't thought about Mom all day, until then. Smooth, beautiful exhaustion massaged every muscle. My thoughts ran clean and clear. I felt good.

I felt *good.*

I felt tired, dirty and honest, and every ache and flutter felt true and justified.

I thought of Mom and kept her at bay, even as I started the car and headed in her direction.

She slithered back into my life, of course, like a wet, wicked snake. I fought back with random thoughts, the most prominent being I wouldn't get home early enough to get the Trans Am.

The car: I hated it without emotion, if such a thing were possible.

One more day, I told myself, easing my old Le Mans into traffic. I told myself I was too tired to fuck, but I knew it wasn't true, and I gave another round to the snake woman.

Insidious whore.

I stopped at a fast food restaurant and ordered garbage. I shoveled French fries and grease into my body as I maneuvered the car through post rush hour traffic.

Loud music tore my speakers apart. I drew in natural, farm fresh air and let the music rip layers of my life away. I smiled all the way home. I relished my life, chaotic and corrupt as it was, until I turned the corner at the top of the driveway and saw the car:

The Trans Am.

She must have had it delivered.

... in my normal parking place.

I had no choice except to park my car off to the side, backed up on a spot of dirt by the house's propane tank. I killed the engine and glared at the Trans Am forty feet away.

What had I been thinking?

I remembered fucking her while she coerced my dad into buying the damned thing. I remembered filling her ass with cum and laughing at her, at Dad, at all of it. I wasn't laughing now.

Sick fuck, I named myself and pushed open the car door. The sun beat low and hard off the horizon, reflecting burnt orange light off everything, including the beautiful new car.

Mom would be thrilled about the car, I knew, as I cut through the garage to the house. But shame and embarrassment slowed my hand to the doorknob. I pictured her waiting all day, brewing excitement in a cup of ecstasy. Hours she waited to revel in our success, in our grand and glorious game.

Stop, I thought, just stop, pause and take a fucking breath.

No harm done: it's just a car.

I opened the door and found her standing in front of me, naked from the waist down in high heels, of course. She was my mother. I wouldn't have her any other way. She wore a long, loose fitting blouse belted at her waist and draped to her bare mound. She threw her arms around my neck and kissed me with such depth and intensity I couldn't resist.

My fingers slid down her back, down further and inside. I found without surprise she'd lubricated herself, prepared herself for me – for her reward for the car.

She moaned and stood up on her toes, leaning into me, rocking and swaying her hips, moving just right for my fingers to sink deep into her.

I was filthy from work, but she wouldn't release me. Mom ran her hands through my dirty hair and ground her hips into me. "You saw it," she hissed with a wet voice in my ear.

Again, she kissed me hard, thrusting her hips into me, running her hands up and down my back and releasing one soft, animal moan after another. "Fuck me, Jack," she hissed again. "Fuck me as hard as you can...."

Mom shoved her hand down my pants and brutally rubbed my cock. "Hurt me, Jack," she said in a soft and tangled voice, stroking my immediate hard on. "Hurt me with it," she snarled when I didn't reply. Her eyes flared and her body wrapped around me like a python.

I grabbed her hair and yanked her head back, straining her neck and exposing her jugular vein. I yanked again and felt the pressure of her scalp.

She dug her claws into my flesh. I yanked her head back a third time and violence locked us together. Mom purred and smiled wickedly through dark, almost black eyes.

Rapid, brutal sex filled my lungs and burned like oil in my belly. The scent of her boiled my blood. The taste of her fueled my attack. I fell upon her with insanity and lust, ripped her cunt open and destroyed myself inside her.

Mom screamed and sobbed openly, begging her god for mercy and pain. She clawed at the floor with broken fingernails and shook the house with cruel, unfettered cries.

I punched her full-fist to the side of the head and screamed for death and silence. She cried for more and begged me to stop. I slapped her and beat her until my body failed and she lay red-faced and bleeding at my feet.

"Open your mouth," I said without consideration.

She obeyed with visible hunger in her eyes.

I filled her with piss and tears and watched her squirm in her own vomit.

Next.

I didn't know. I scattered the puzzle pieces and didn't care anymore.

"Clean yourself up," I said without interest. "We're going for a ride in the car."

I left her like a piece of shit on the dining room floor and headed for the main bathroom.

Sudden curiosity turned me around and I found her curled into a ball on the floor, panting and slowly catching her breath. "Okay," she answered quietly, absently reaching out to me. "I love you," she said then, as if she wondered at the words.

"Stupid bitch," I replied and walked away.

Mom cried openly and folded tighter in on herself. She cast a broken child's cry into the night – a cry of shame and humiliation, of embarrassment and fear. I stood in the bathroom and listened to her wail into eternity the destruction of her life.

I showered without memory of it and found her on the edge of the bed. She absently touched her face and brushed her hair aside. Her green eyes flared and winked into darkness. Devastation and horror framed her features, and I imagined fear defined her heart.

I lifted her sticky chin with one finger and met her halfway to sympathy. "It's okay," I told her. "Just clean yourself up and we'll go for a ride."

She sniffled like a little girl and cast an embarrassed smile at me. "Okay," she said quietly. She stood up, and I was surprised at how small and frail she was without the heels on. "I love you, Jack," she said tentatively, in an honest search for acknowledgment.

A little girl, I thought, watching her sheepishly wait for my reply – a frightened little girl who had no idea how to save herself.

"I love you, too," I said, knowing it to be true.

I knew every word of it to be sadly, pathetically true.

Chapter 15

I didn't fuck her in the Trans Am the first night we had it.

And I knew full well *we* had the car.

Our car.

I didn't fuck her again because I was goddamned tired from both work and using her as a sexual punching bag when I got home. Despite the agony I had put her through only an hour before, she obviously expected sex on our maiden voyage. I had to explain to her three times why I didn't fuck her on the side of the road, somewhere in the dark, on a goddamned Thursday night.

Mom played every bit the needy child and thankless whore. I claimed her as an animal, as a pet, as a bitch on a leash. Which end of the leash, I had no idea, and it didn't matter.

We'd each grown accustomed to the cruelty of it all, the brutality, the humiliation and degradation – and we expected it, anticipated and demanded the animal inside of each other.

Mom played every bit the needy mother and thankless wife. I roamed the house with a perpetual stomachache and found no relief from the images in my mind. But nothing stopped me from fucking her two, three, sometimes four times a day.

She had become my drug of choice and I overdosed willingly and with intention.

What intention, I had no idea.

"I'm not selling the Le Mans," I told her, wondering at the ridiculous conversation. Rain poured outside and I let it destroy Saturday morning.

Mom pouted.

She fucking pouted and I would have slapped her had I not known she'd enjoy it.

"The Le Mans is in my name," I explained for the eighth time. "The Trans Am is in your name. It's your car –"

"It's *your* car," she insisted, almost ready to cry.

Over this?

"Okay," I said, pushing away my half eaten breakfast. "It's my car. But I'm not selling the Le Mans."

She folded her hands in her lap and crossed her ankles beneath her chair. New shoes again, black, strapped, high and tight. She'd snapped both heels off her beige shoes the night I fucked her on the dining room floor and pissed down her throat.

I liked the new shoes better anyway. The straps went partway up her calves and the tall heel made her stagger when she walked. I allowed a smile when I remembered her buying them with Dad's credit card.

I didn't give a shit anymore – or so I told myself. My stomach tightened and released at odd intervals but I knew it didn't matter. I just didn't give a shit. Either way.

We had fucked liked lovers the rest of the night – last night – and in the morning we woke up in each others arms.

I missed the simplicity as I sat listening to the rain – the ease of simply fucking her, then ignoring her as she cooked and cleaned around me.

As her feet bobbed under the chair and she pouted about the future of my old car, nights like last night fell further from the truth.

"I should have bought the white ones, too," she said, stirring me back. "For when we go out." She unfolded herself from the chair and stretched her legs out, tilting and twirling her shoes. "These won't go with my summer stuff."

I wondered why I didn't find that last one funny.

Mom wore only a thin, black robe, loosely tied and open to reveal her shaved cunt. Her tits hung full and heavy, nipples hard, erect and easily pushing through the veiled material.

I stood without consideration, pulled my cock out of my pajamas and watched absently as she sucked me off with grateful enthusiasm. She only squirmed a few times and she didn't spill a drop.

"We should go back and get them," I offered as I slipped myself away and took my seat.

She smiled as I poured us each another cup of coffee. She leaned in and landed a quick kiss on my cheek. "I want to buy something sexy for you, too," she said, staying close an extra moment. "I want to be sexy for you, Jack."

"You are," I offered, sipping coffee and marveling at people's remarkable ability to adapt to any fucked up shit that came their way.

She smiled and again I was reminded of a giddy school girl praised for a successful assignment. "I love you so much," she said, dripping with acid truth. She stood before I could respond and cleared the table.

"Can we go get the shoes?" she asked from the kitchen.

I watched the rain, suddenly unable to wreck the day, and forgot to answer.

"Can we?"

I picked up and held the nervous tone in her voice. She responded so quickly to my slightest remarks, my tone, my silence, my every sound and movement.

"I can get the shoes and something sexy for you," she said, reinforcing her offer. "I want to buy something for you, too," she added, now close to pleading.

Mom was exhausting, I admitted to myself, watching her suffer a moment longer before telling her, "Yes."

I would be hurting her again tonight, I decided. I smelled it on her, the craving, the desire, the absolute need for mind altering abuse.

We were each others drug of choice, I reminded myself, dismissing and rearranging as many thoughts as it took to quiet my stomach and mind. I found myself standing naked in the bedroom, aware only when I noticed her leaning in the doorway and smiling at me.

"Do you want to fuck before we go, Jackie?" she asked, only half laughing at the sight. "Is that what you're trying to tell me?"

I ignored her but couldn't hide my smile. "When we get home," I said without looking at her. I dug in the dresser and took too long to pick underwear.

She sprang off the doorway and kissed me quick on the cheek before I could blink. "I can't wait," she whispered in my ear.

Immediate stomach pain flashed and passed. I told myself things were beginning to mellow between us. I told myself the relationship stabilized even as I pulled her over by her hips and ran my hand up her thigh.

She balanced herself on my shoulder, stood up on her toes and ran her hand through my hair. She moaned and squirmed for me, spread her legs for me and dug her nails into my scalp.

I pinched her clit, held her in place and told myself everything worked out fine. I thrust my fingers into her and pressed her asshole with my thumb.

"That's nice," she moaned, gyrating her hips and curling her claws in my hair. "You're so good to me, Jackie...."

Yes, I thought, teasing and twisting her clit and holding her ass while a mild orgasm washed over her. I released her and let her squirm against me for a moment.

Everything worked out fine, I thought, slipping a shirt over my head and turning to find her across the hall. Mom squatted on the toilet and offered a shy, submissive smile.

That's your fucking mother. The words ripped out of my chest and left me hollow inside, so much so that I touched my chest to make sure there wasn't a Mom-sized hole through my heart. A sharp, bright vibration slipped down my spine and stopped me solid.

Motherfucker.

You don't just fuck her, you abuse the living shit out of her.

You piss on your own mother.

You cum in her mouth and wash it down with piss.

What the hell and why?

Sick fuck, sick fuck.

A childrens song soft in the background.

Sick whore fuck, dancing on the sand.

...?

Everything instantly and simultaneously smashed all the words – all my thoughts and feelings and childrens magic – mangled and garbled in a perfectly understandable mess.

She wiped her ass and flushed the toilet and I thought an hour had passed. "Are you alright?" she asked with a moment of concern.

I nodded and watched her cunt disappear as she pulled her dress down.

She named it cunt and threw it at you.

She gave it to me like a birthday present.

Here's my cunt, sweetheart.

Fire at will.

Mom stepped in view and looked through me – or maybe I looked through her. Either way, she forced me to look at her storm-green eyes and listen when she asked again if I was okay. "We don't have to go if you don't feel good," she added with apparent concern.

"No," I replied too quickly. "No. I'm fine. I want to go."

Proud of yourself?

A blurry ricochet of images, thoughts and emotions collided and slammed against each other: A manic, mental traffic pileup repeated itself in my mind.

"Honey?" she asked, again forcing me to look at her. The devil in her eyes smiled back and, for the first time, I feared for my sanity.

Piss drinking whore.

I named it all bullshit for the sake of survival and smiled down at her. I ran my hand down her back, pushed up her dress and rubbed the meat of her bare ass.

She moaned into my chest and squirmed for me. "I like that," she whispered as if I cared.

I slid a quick finger into her dry cunt, toyed with her asshole and released her. "Let's go," I said, still feeling the distinct mark of a strange separation.

Then, "Wait," I blurted, stopping her in her tracks.

I took her purse, opened it without a word, and removed the KY. She smiled, lifted her dress, and said nothing. I squeezed out more than necessary and worked her cunt and asshole into a liquid frenzy.

"Fuck me," she said, or something equally inane.

"No," I replied as if answering a child. I pushed my thumb deep into her ass and worked her cunt wide with three fingers before releasing her.

She wobbled once or twice before regaining her balance. "I want to get the shoes first, anyway," she blurted, then continued to prattle on as if words could save her.

I heard blah, blah, blah as I drove into the suburbs toward the shopping mall. Every stop light found my fingers inside her. She gave up pulling her dress down and closing her legs. She fingered herself for most of the ride down, only letting go when we stopped.

"I want to fuck so bad, Jackie," she said too loudly at one light. I looked over and found a mother and teenage daughter glaring at us from the next car. My mother the whore turned back to me and, without missing a beat, said even louder, "Pull over somewhere and fuck me."

I berated her like a child but found it difficult to ignore my own sudden hard on. She ignored me, took my hand, and masturbated herself furiously as we drove away.

By the time I parked the car, she'd had one orgasm and told me she loved me four times. She reeked of fresh, wet sex, palpable even in the store. Mom took my hand and led me directly to the shoe department.

I smiled when I saw the same saleswoman from before look up and frown.

Mom knew what she wanted, I gave her that much anyway.

We walked out of the mall listening to the soft click of her new white shoes. She took my arm and squeezed our bodies together. "You could fuck me right here," she whispered up at me. "In front of everyone."

I barely missed a beat and kept on walking.

"You can do anything you want to me, Jack. Anytime you want."

She released me then and walked happily beside me. The smell of sex lay thick around us. Chaotic images exploded across my brain, this time leaving only confusion, fear and guilt.

Liar, I heard somewhere in the distance.

Saint.

I took my time in the busy parking lot. I smiled when I saw an old couple stop and wait for my spot. I looked down at Mom and crossed my arms over the open roof. "Lean forward."

She jerked and looked up as if I startled her. I unzipped her dress and said nothing. We were parked near the door in a great spot on a busy day. People constantly walked passed us. Cars struggled around the old couple, hungry for my precious parking space.

I kept her car door open and said, "Lift your dress and spread your legs," with a smile.

She sat up straight and looked around, obviously taking note of the constant passersby. Mom pulled her dress up slowly and spread her legs, looking up at me only after revealing her full slit.

"Open your purse."

"Jack, are you going to –"

"Shh. Open your purse."

Mom moved so quickly in and out of her purse, she had three fingers full of KY into her cunt before I blinked twice. "OhmyGodJack," she hissed out of her mouth as she worked herself open for me. Almost everyone who passed by looked at us and could clearly see what she was doing.

I smiled at them all and climbed in on top of her, leaving the door open on purpose. In one motion, I unzipped my pants and slid my cock into her. I dug my fingers into her hips and positioned her on the seat. We immediately fell into a hard, swift rhythm. I fucked her harder and she drove her hips up into me with equal ferocity.

I stretched back and grabbed the open roof, increasing my pace and rocking the car steadily. A few people stopped and watched. I looked down at Mom and found her staring up at me, flushed, wide eyed and strained under my relentless assault.

She opened her mouth and tried to speak, or changed her mind, or something else. I told her to lift her arms up. She obeyed and stuck them through the open roof. I slid her dress off in one smooth motion and immediately resumed fucking her.

Mom drew a sharp breath at the abrupt act and complete exposure. Before she blinked, I pulled her forward, unsnapped her bra and tossed it into the back seat.

"You're a fucking piece of shit whore," I said without malice in a voice loud enough for our small audience to hear.

"I love you," she said back to me, holding back tears.

I pounded my cock into her as hard as I absolutely could.

Mom grunted and groaned under the assault. She looked up at me with thick, wet mascara smeared around her eyes and said, "I love you," again, as if it mattered.

As if anything mattered.

I grunted and blew my load into her, pulled out and let the rest splatter across her belly. I climbed off and out of the car and did my best to casually slide behind the steering wheel and drive away.

Mom did her best to cover her naked body behind sunglasses and sweat. "Can I put my dress back on?" she made the mistake of asking.

"No," I replied without explanation and kept my eyes on the road.

"I love you," she said, tentatively.

"Shut up," I replied, rubbing her head like a dog.

She cried quietly the rest of the way home and I didn't blame her.

Chapter 16

I didn't remember the night before. I wasn't missing pieces or struggling to fill in blanks. The entire night was a blank. Somewhere I'd lost a good twelve hours.

Mom's fat lip and black eye indicated a typical evening at home. She snored like a pig and lay twisted in a mess of stained sheets and flesh. Assorted bruises covered her body, none of which I remembered inflicting and all of which I knew were mine.

I got up to piss and discovered the toilet seat in the middle of the hallway.

Then I remembered booze.

Mom and her scotch and water. Me and my Seven and Sevens.

And pot.

Fuck, I had pot. I found a big roach in her ashtray, lit it and released a sigh. Every muscle and bone in my body screamed in pain. Even my cock hurt, which did nothing to prevent the ritual morning hard-on.

Mom grunted, stopped snoring and rolled on to her back. I pulled the tangled sheet off her and thought nothing. She squirmed a bit; then went back to snoring. I wondered what day it was and stared at the bruises covering her belly – and arms, tits, neck, thighs, too many to count. Her face looked like I beat her with a closed fist.

My cock was so hard, it hurt. Of course.

I hit the roach a few times and found the KY under the bed. I slid Mom into position and climbed on top of her. She hadn't been *Mom* in months – and the thought almost made me laugh out loud. *Mom, woman, bitch, whore, slut, cunt, skank*, neither one of us cared anymore. We'd run out of words a long time ago.

I slowly fucked her and listened to her snore. She moaned a few times and spread her legs a bit, but she pretty much laid there while I masturbated inside of her. Afterward, I threw the sheet across her, found my bag of weed and headed for the coffee pot.

I thought again of her bruises and knew I wouldn't give her a break today. I was going to hurt her again, because I *wanted* to hurt her again.

And, somehow, I knew she wanted me to hurt her. Like last night, *somehow*, inside my *self* – or something equally inane and self-serving – she pushed my buttons and worked my levers. She begged for pain – but more than that, though: Pain was only a by-product, a placeholder, a memory stamp – or *fuck this*. I'd given myself a headache and found myself fumbling with the coffee pot.

Or was I making it all up? I watched the coffee brew and second guessed myself. My cock was rock hard again, of course, and why not? Fuck, I wished I remembered at least *some* of last night. My stomach tensed and tightened and I discovered a new hole in my guts.

Me, then. Me? Right now, I thought. Pick up where I left off. *Fuck that bitch. She wasn't the one who stopped last night. She fucked* me *until I passed out. Bullshit.*

Bullshit.

The sudden and sustained urge to go in and continue beating my mother terrified me. I wanted to beat her so badly... so badly. To punch her and kick her, slap her, spit on her, piss on her, shit on her and flush her down the toilet.....

My cock was so fucking hard it didn't feel human.

I didn't feel human.

One sip of coffee told me I forgot the cream. The bitter taste reminded me of Dad. Images of him walking through the door forced me to turn around even though I knew he wasn't there.

From inside, I beat him.

From inside, I raped him.

I vomited one sip of coffee and the liquid mess from last night on to the kitchen floor. My hands shook, my eyes watered and my brain revved up to an immediate, insane pace; then shut down.

My brain just shut down, or, I didn't know. I just shut down.

Whatever. I found myself wiping up the last of the mess. Time, then. Gone.

Poof.

I had just done this. I had just thrown up in the kitchen. I knew it had just happened.

Seconds ago.

I pitched the last of the paper towel into the trash and reached for the cup of black coffee.

Ice cold.

Seconds ago, I thought again and insisted. *Fine, then. Fine.* I walked to the side door, conscious of every step, and opened it. I half expected to find my dad laying on the garage floor, freshly beaten and raped.

Instead, I found a very normal garage.

So, fuck, what the fuck, and I shut the door. I locked the door –

And found myself in the kitchen, using the same hand, *at the same time,* to open the microwave door and grab the hot cup of coffee I *hadn't put in the microwave yet.*

I cried then, softly and quietly for myself. I just cried, and the faintest, most beautiful relief I'd felt in months washed over me. My infernal cock softened and blood coursed through my veins. I slid back inside myself and cried without shame or regret.

Then, "Jack...?"

She dangled my name like a noose in front of me. *My own fucking name hung like a noose around my neck.* My hand shook once and I watched a few slow motion drops of coffee hit the floor.

"Jackie...?"

I heard the pain in her voice. My hand shook again as I poured the cream. My cock stiffened back into steel despite my best effort, and I lost my tears as if I'd never found them.

"Jackie, sweetheart... please.... Mommy doesn't feel so good...."

I almost squeezed the coffee cup into a million pieces.

Really?

Not really.

I stood in front of her, holding her hand mirror, aiming it at her and wondering where I'd gotten the mirror from, exactly. And then I spit words at her. "Look at yourself," I said, shoving the mirror in front of her swollen, cut and bruised face.

She reached up and lightly touched the worst of the two sides.

I pulled the mirror away and slapped her.

I never heard anyone scream and cry out in such bitter, wretched agony. She collapsed into herself in obvious, horrendous pain. Even muffled into the pillow, her cries filled the room with such heightened agony, I cried over her, above her, and felt no sympathy or relief.

Mom sobbed openly, repeating my name and telling me how much she loved me. She looked up at me and displayed her hideous, monstrous face. Covered in pain and tears, beaten into unnatural form, unrecognizable as my mother, as anyone's mother, she barely looked human.

Then, I raped her.

She kicked and screamed and begged me to stop. Fear, anger, love and lust distorted her twisted face. I held her hips in place and forced my cock into her dry asshole. She curled the bed sheet into her fists and screamed in agony at the top of her lungs.

I held her in place and watched her, studied her, tried to feel something, anything for her – or myself for that matter. I stood still with my cock buried inside of her and waited for her to calm down, to stop screaming and squirming – to accept herself as she was, to accept everything as it was –

"Steady yourself," I heard myself say.

"Jackie...," she said so quietly I had to lean down to her lips to hear. "Please, Jackie," she said. "... please, it hurts...."

I rocked her back and forth, moving us together, remaining motionless inside of her.

She cried again, softly this time, as if with conscious care, with conscious measure. I leaned down again and studied the side of her face, her right eye, exactly, damp, bloodshot, dark puffy skin pushing in around it. I studied her and assessed her as if she wasn't real, as if none of this was real. As if nothing mattered, which it didn't, I either knew or told myself. I couldn't remember.

I slowly fucked my mother's asshole. She cried harder and bit her lip until it bled, begging with green-ice eyes and stale words for me to stop – something, whatever it was I was doing, or had done, or was going to do, to her.

"Oh, Jackie...," she said and faded away, unable to form words from tears.

"You're a dried up old prune," I blurted, suddenly laughing and slapping the side of her ass. A few quick thrusts stopped her reply and brought more tears.

She mumbled something unintelligible, so I fucked her harder. My cock burned down to my balls, so I slapped her face. Her expression locked into a tight, perpetual silent scream. I thrust without rhythm, without thought or concern, and I watched a long string of drool slide from the corner of her stagnant mouth to the sheet beneath her face.

Eventually, she blinked and drew a huge breath. In chaotic misery, we shared the brutality of ourselves and of our lost intention. She winced painfully with each thrust. I examined every hair on her head.

A feeble orgasm overtook me and I ejaculated nothing inside of her. I pulled out and stood waiting for a response.

Mom cried quietly, face buried in the dirty sheets. She didn't thank me or tell me she loved me. She didn't turn around and smile wickedly at me. She didn't zero in on me with her dirty green eyes.

She said nothing when I dressed, brought her coffee or asked if she wanted anything. She hadn't moved since I pulled my cock out of her ass. Mom bunched her shoulders and neck together, kept her face down in the sheets and covered whatever might be visible with both hands.

I didn't know what to do, so I cleaned the garage with nervous energy and confusion, finding the combination ineffective against detail. I swept some parts of the floor twice, some parts not at all. I put away *almost* everything good and threw away *almost* everything bad. I paid extreme attention to some tasks and barely anything to others. In between cigarettes and moments of confusion, I checked on her to see if she was awake, to see if I'd hurt her physically – to make sure she was still goddamn alive.

She lay in the same place, same position, same everything.

So I cleaned, more or less, the same everything.

Over and over.

Hours.

"What?" I finally asked, having run out of everything. I stood in the bedroom doorway and knew she wasn't asleep. "What, Mom?" I asked, preparing to turn away from her again. A slow shiver coursed her spine and she stirred like a serpent in slow motion.

I stepped into the room and knelt by her head. I pushed her hair aside and her hands shook. A heavy blue bruise covered half her face. Her head lifted suddenly, then dropped, startling me for an instant.

Jesus, I thought, and wondered if I should take her to the hospital.

"Jackie...?" she mouthed my name more than said it. "What happened?"

I shook my head slowly and brushed her hair with my fingers. "I don't know," I admitted, finally looking her in the eye. "I don't remember."

Her eyes closed and she feigned a smile. "It hurts, Jackie," she said from a distance, resting her head back down on the bed.

"What, Mom?" I asked, feeling my stomach twist into knots. "What hurts?" Mild panic sat beside my belly ache.

What if I had to take her to the hospital? What was I supposed to say? This is my Mom. I beat and raped her last night. Can you fix her up so I can do it again?

Fuck.

Rape.

"Everything hurts," she said in a clear voice. Mom reached out weakly and touched my arm. She smiled, sort of, in obvious pain. Green eyes suddenly in focus, she adjusted her position and touched my face. "Don't be afraid, sweetheart," she said, clearing her throat with the words. "I'm alright. Momma's alright."

Momma's alright.

I stood up and slowly pulled the sheet off her, revealing her naked body sprawled across the bed. "Roll over," I said with mild authority.

She obeyed without a word, wincing only once on the way over. "Yes, Jack," she added with sore humor in her voice. Then, without looking at me, "You didn't do anything I didn't want you to do."

Fuck you, I thought. I asked her if she remembered last night.

"Some of it," she replied, then closed her eyes to think. "Parts," she said, opening her eyes and smiling at me. She stretched her naked body out and tried to make light of her pain. Mom looked old, tired, worn out and every bit her fifty-seven years.

"You called me a prune this morning," she said with a smile, leaving the statement open.

I winced inside. "Yes," I said, adding nothing and feeling my blood thicken. She didn't need medical attention, which made her available to me, *in my mind*, for further abuse. Horrific images of her splattered and splayed across every corner of my mind the instant I realized she was physically okay.

Even as I told myself I would clean her and care for her wounds – or at least leave her the hell alone – I mounted her and drove her to tears again. I drove her with cruelty and malice, and I remembered every second of it when I finished.

She didn't get out of bed until the following afternoon. For two days after, she moved in obvious discomfort and pain.

I let her heal on the outside, at least.

Chapter 17

"I love you," I said, and I meant it. I did love her. In every odd fucking way there was, I loved her. I didn't understand the meaning of the phrase, exactly, but in my heart as I felt it, I loved her.

Mom answered me with a nervous, tentative smile and continued clearing the dinner table. Then, she replied off-cue, "I love you, too, Jack," from the kitchen with her back to me.

The more I took away her humanity, the more I loved her. I watched her move about the kitchen, ignoring me and avoiding my gaze.

Then she looked me in the eye and made a liar out of me. "If I can get into the beauty shop this afternoon, will you take me?" She turned away without expression and continued scrubbing the counter.

"Please," she added as an afterthought.

"Okay," I replied without a second thought.

It occurred to me, then, to actually *look* at her. A week had passed since I found the toilet seat in the hallway. She kept herself clean, avoided makeup, pulled her hair back in a ponytail and wore nothing except one of my dirty work shirts and her new white shoes. Mom created her own version of sexy and smelled like the inside of a work van.

Perfect, I thought. "What about the bruises?" I asked.

"Swelling mostly," she answered with ease. She hesitated but didn't look up from the counter. "The rest I can cover with makeup." She shrugged at the wrong time and ended with an awkward gesture.

"What?" I asked, realizing I wasn't listening to her.

Mom stopped scrubbing and held onto the pad with her long, yellow rubber gloves. "You haven't touched me in a week," she said, still not looking at me. Then, again, the ill-timed shrug. "A week today."

I wondered why she changed the subject, but I didn't ask.

She pushed the pad across the counter, released it and looked at me. "I love what you did to me the other night," she said. Then, she blurted, "I know I cried and asked you to stop, Jack –," and cut herself off in the same breath.

Then she bit her lip.

She bit her lip *and stuck her hip out.*

Please, I thought. *No more words.*

Mom touched her cheek, softly caressing herself and losing herself for an instant. "I like the bruises...." She absently reached for the scrub pad and continued, "I like the pain. Waking up in it, feeling it all over... feeling you all over me."

Mom stopped talking, pushed a stray red hair out of her face and went back to scrubbing the counter.

I sat and studied her, examined her every movement in detail and went out of my way to consciously penetrate her. Scattered, nervous energy vibrated down to her bones.

"Oh," she said then, startling us both. "I have to call the beauty shop." And she did, tossing pad and gloves into the sink and grabbing the phone. Within minutes I discovered we had to leave in a few more minutes – and she was off the phone and scrambling to assemble herself for delivery.

"I'll be in the car," I called out, hearing her faint acknowledgment as I reached for the doorknob.

As I removed the t-tops from the Trans Am, a sudden, low level fear arrived and sat in my belly. I winced and knew she'd wear a babushka. I told myself to remember to put the roof back together and use the air conditioner for the ride home.

She wants to go the beauty shop so I'll touch her again. She likes the pain. She likes the bruises. She likes waking up with me all over her.

I opened the trunk and found myself sitting behind the steering wheel, the engine idling and Mom sliding into the passenger seat.

She wore mostly white to match her shoes, plus big sunglasses, big smile, flower print babushka. "I'm not wearing panties," she announced, struggling with the seat belt.

I faked a smile and said nothing. My stomach twisted, but I couldn't resist the urge to get out of the car and check if the roof sections were stowed in the trunk.

They were.

Of course.

"Everything okay?" Mom asked.

Everything was okay. "Yes."

I'd removed the roof sections, stowed them away and started the car – and I remembered none of it. I turned and found her next to me, or me next to her – not outside the car by the trunk, but inside the car. So, I smiled.

I smiled and squeezed her knee and kissed her cheek. I told her she looked great in many ways and that I loved her in many more. We drove to the beauty shop in silence until the last mile.

"Everything is alright, Jack," Mom said, as if she understood some great truth. I shrugged inwardly. Maybe she did.

"I love everything you do to me," she continued when I didn't say anything. "I love making you happy."

I almost pulled over to the side of the road and puked. *Fucking whore* was my second thought, although I wasn't sure which one of us I meant. My cock was hard as a rock and my emotions splashed around like a helpless, drowning child. I had to ask her twice for directions to the beauty shop.

She remained quiet until we arrived, then I don't know what the hell happened.

"Jane!" a woman's voice screeched.

My neck twisted hard to the left.

"Renee!" Mom fired back.

Back hard to the right and I felt pinned down by a hail of gunfire. The two women hugged like old friends or enemies or both. Mom, short and fleshy and Renee, tall and thin, wrapped around each other like a snake and a mongoose gone mad. Love, hate, I couldn't tell the difference and wondered if there was one.

"Can you make me sexy, Renee, darling?"

Good God.

"You're already sexy, darling," Renee answered without missing a beat. "But I can make you irresistible."

Renee looked about ten years younger than Mom, and she was dark everywhere Mom was light.

Mom, I thought and left it hang. What the hell was I doing here?

I opened my mouth to ask how long it takes to make sexy people irresistible when they both turned on me.

Renee aimed and fired, "And who is this gorgeous young man?" She extended her long thin hand and flashed numerous fake eye lashes at me.

Mom touched my shoulder and I jumped.

They both smiled like vampires, and I concentrated everything on remaining in place and not running for the door.

"Jac –" I said, failing to get my name out.

"This is my son," Mom said, squeezing my shoulder and presenting me for display. "This is my Jack. Isn't he gorgeous?"

"Delicious," Renee added, continuing to hold my hand. "Gorgeous and delicious, and I could eat him up on the spot."

Mom slipped her arm around my waist and pulled me close. "He's mine!" she snapped playfully. "Now, make me sexy, sexy, sexy!"

My cheeks flushed and they both laughed.

"Jane, darling, are you putting dirty thoughts in your son's head? About his own mother? Nasty girl! Nasty!"

"Shh, darling," Mom said, digging her nails into my arm, then releasing me. "It's a secret."

They laughed again and discarded me, walking away arm in arm.

"Two hours." Renee turned back and smiled at me. "Make it three hours. Come get your mother in three hours, and you won't be able to keep your hands off her."

And... they laughed, of course.

"Nasty!"

I would have shot them both if I'd had a gun.

Three other hair stylists and three other clients, each in various stages of assembly, all stared at me as if expecting *Act Two*. I slunk back to the Trans Am and realized I had no idea what to do for three hours.

I could use it to get three hours the fuck out of town, a voice in back of my mind said, as if it knew I wouldn't listen; as if it knew I wouldn't even try to save myself. I found myself in the arcade parking lot when I couldn't even remember starting the car. White knuckle fear held my hands to the steering wheel and tossed cannonballs around in my stomach.

I leaned out the window to puke and heard Dave's voice cut a hole through the shit that was my brain.

"Man! What the hell with the Trans Am?" he said, appearing like magic and resting his arms on the cut away roof. He smiled down at me with too blonde hair. "Smokey and the fucking bandit, man. Holy shit."

When I left the air empty between us, he added, "Where the hell you been?" as if his presence alone wasn't enough to push me over the edge.

I'm fucking my mother, I heard myself say from somewhere. *Put a gun to my head, brother. You can have the car.*

"Man, Jack, you okay?" Dave asked as his smile straightened out.

And I like fucking her, I said, or thought, and whatever anyway, it was all the same. *All I do is fuck her. All I think about is fucking her. All I want to do is fuck her. Dave, why can't you fucking hear me? I can't keep my cock out of her!*

"Dave, do you fucking hear me? I can't keep my cock out of her!"

But he wasn't there. Nobody was there. The arcade wasn't open this early, and the entire parking lot was empty, save for me and *the car*.

Fuck.

Fuck, shit, piss, and I looked at the clock. Four minutes. Four minutes since I found myself in the parking lot. I looked down the road and saw the highway entrance sign. Half a mile down the road and the whole world opened up for me – or would open up if I let it.

Start the car. Start the goddamned car.

Get. The fuck. Out of there.

I put my hand on my knee to keep it from shaking. Decide now, I thought. The middle ground was killing me.

So, I did.

Two hours and fifty-six minutes later, I held her hand on the way home and told her she looked sexy in many different ways. Mom crossed her legs and let her skirt ride up. "I'm not bad for an old prune," she said with a smile and meant it.

"I'd fuck you," I replied from deep inside my stomach. We both laughed, I turned up the air conditioner and pushed eighty miles an hour on the way home.

She looked and smelled expensive and cheap at the same time. Hair, fingernails, toenails, makeup, Renee slathered on the works.

Mom walked out of the place with a bag full of products she'd probably never use.

I pulled up by the garage, turned off the engine and held her in place when she reached for the door handle. She shivered once and pulled her leg up a touch further, pushed her skirt up a touch higher and squeezed my hand a touch harder.

I peeled my hand out of hers and felt angry then, suddenly, without cause. I unzipped my pants and let my cock spring to immediate attention.

"Suck my dick," I heard myself say, spitting the words at her. "Whore."

Within minutes I destroyed everything Renee had created. Everything except her fingernails, oddly enough, though I knew they wouldn't survive the rest of the day.

I felt Mom try and help me. I felt her fight herself, struggle with herself, argue with herself to stay loose, stay open and to let me have my brutal way with her.

But she failed us both at every turn.

I crumpled a huge chunk of her hair in my hand, pumped my cock down her throat and laughed at her. I laughed at her. She gagged and snorted, spit up and choked. I thrust my hips up and fucked her stupid fucking face.

Her body tensed and stiffened in every direction. She reflexively tried to pull away several times and she dug her fingernails into my thigh. Her right leg straightened and pushed hard against the car's floor.

We both heard the heal of her shoe snap. She gasped and went limp in surrender, though she still struggled for air. I thrust wildly into her for a few more seconds, tightened my grip in her hair, and filled her mouth with cum.

My body heaved and released as if I hadn't taken a breath in days. Mom panted like an animal in my lap and hungrily slurped and licked my cock clean.

Mom.

Good God.

I pulled her up by her hair and held her to my face. She looked like an animal, like a monster, worse, better. I didn't know and didn't give a shit. She squeezed mascara stained tears out of her bloodshot eyes and tried to smile. Her wet mouth curled into a lipstick-smeared mess. I rubbed some stray cum off her cheek and pushed my thumb into her mouth.

She sucked my thumb like a baby.

"You make me sick," I said, getting out of the car.

"I love you," she said, and she meant it.

Chapter 18

I wished for a five day blackout and instead remembered every detail. Like punishment, my memories, perpetual torture on endless film.

I duct taped a black plastic garbage bag over the bathroom window and thought myself sane. I did the same thing to the kitchen window, although I did a better job of measuring and cutting to fit the plastic around the window frame. Nobody actually used the front door so I nailed it shut, literally.

"Shit," I said for no reason.

"You okay, Jackie?" Mom called from the bedroom. "What are you doing? What are you hammering?"

Fine, I thought. I'm fine. I thought I said the words. I *knew* I said them.

"Jack?"

Or not, either way. Next, the dining room window. "Stay in the bedroom," I said, tasting my words this time so I knew I said them aloud. I cut up more plastic bags and taped them together.

"Jack, I have to go to the bathroom."

Not yet. No. "I'll be there in a few minutes." No. Not yet.

"Jack. Please."

"No, goddamnit." I looked at the pointed scissors and told myself I wouldn't kill her. "I'll be there in a few minutes. Now, shut up."

"Okay...."

I taped the long piece of plastic to the dining room window and sealed the edges.

Dark. Everything had to be dark. I couldn't take the sun, the light, not anymore. I just couldn't take it anymore and fuck the sun, anyway.

Sun. *Son.* Ha. Fuck.

"I really have to pee, Jack...."

"Then pee," I growled, chasing my eyes to the scissors on the floor. "Piss all over yourself, I don't give a shit. Just shut the hell up for a few minutes."

Silence, then, though not forever and again I ignored my impulse.

I drew the heavy drapes in the family and living room. I closed the blinds and shut the doors to the other two bedrooms. I fumbled for the light switch on the hallway wall. Outside, it was a little past noon. Inside, there was no time.

No more time.

Dark, black stale night crept in from every corner and slithered in from every crack.

I could breathe now, I told myself. I could breathe.

I stared down at Mom and couldn't deny her sheepish grin. She'd pissed all over herself and the bed. "You didn't come and untie me, Jack," she said, slowly picking up tone and tempo. "I told you I had to go. I didn't know what to do. I tried to hold it, Jack, but –"

"It's okay," I said, cutting her twine bindings with a steak knife. She unfolded herself from the wet mess. I pointed to the bathroom and said, "Go," before she opened her mouth.

She scurried like a rabbit and called back, "Jack? What's going on? Why is there plastic over all the –"

"Clean yourself up," I replied while stripping the bed. "And don't be all day about it."

"Yes, Jack."

"And keep the door open."

"Yes, Jack."

"And bring me a clean, dry washcloth."

"Yes, Jack."

"Did I tell you to be quick about it?"

"Yes, Jack."

Running water and ruffling towels filled the new silence between us. Refracted bathroom light drew misshapen shadows on the wall behind the bed. In one I saw myself laughing back at me, or smiling at least, or pointing a finger at me, or turning away in disgust.

I turned away and deposited the dirty sheets in the laundry closet down the hallway, to be ignored like everything else house related.

When I returned a moment later, Mom stood naked in the bedroom, staring at mattress stains. "I'll get some new sheets," she said, turning to leave.

"No," I said, stopping her retreat. I looked around the dresser and found my cigarettes and lighter and lit us each one.

"Jack, we need sheets," she said quietly, accepting the cigarette. She took a long drag with a shaking hand and shuffled from one foot to the other.

"What?" I asked.

"Nothing."

I blew cigarette smoke at her. "Tell me."

A stream of words poured out of her without pause or punctuation. "I'm a little scared I love this I mean please don't take this the wrong way I love this I love where this is going I want this so bad Jackie but I'm scared I'm just scared –"

Then, one breath and, "You know?"

I understood scared. "Get on the bed, face down. You can put the sheets on later."

She hesitated. "Jackie, I –"

"Don't be afraid," I said without looking at her, without touching her, without physically engaging her. "Now, get on the bed."

She rubbed her arms and stood up on her toes, then down, twice. "It's cold in here, Jackie."

"Not for long," I replied, taking her elbow and gently leading her the two steps to the bed. I released her and drew a silent breath.

She turned and sat on the edge of the bed before I could say anything. She looked so small, sitting there in the dark on the dirty, stained mattress. For an instant, her phosphorescent eyes cut through the darkness and bore deep into me. I saw her inside, felt her from somewhere else inside, from a place and space *not here*.

From *there*, then, a place inside and far away, I saw my mother real and fresh, true baked love and cookies. I saw her fresh best pearls and rings, Dad's favorite pumpkin pie and her photogenic, effervescent smile.

So, "Mom," I said and lost it all in an instant.

"I want you to hurt me, Jackie."

So, I did.

I managed five awkward, ill-timed slaps to her face as she scrambled away and assumed a face down position. I put one knee on her ass, pressed a hand down on the back of her head and buried her face in the mattress.

I held her down until she thought her end was near and erupted into a weak, knowing resistance. I released her head, and her face sprang up for air. She pushed herself to her elbows and drank in the air around her.

I pushed off her, off the bed, and reached for the roll of twine I'd found in the garage. She didn't say a word or move a muscle when I tied her, as she was, to the four corners of the bed. Elbows and wrists toward the head, knees and ankles back.

"You have slack," I said, looking at her, at what I had done and wondering what I would do in such a position. "Up on your elbows like that. You have slack."

She said nothing and I shrugged as I set the roll on the dresser. I picked up the washcloth she'd brought from the bathroom and one of my neckties I'd worn twice in the last three years. I fashioned a crude blindfold and asked her if it was too tight.

"It's perfect," she said, and I believed her.

I silently cursed us both and picked up my leather belt.

"Jack...?" she inquired and I laid the belt gently across her back.

"Thank you," she corrected when she discovered what I was about.

I slid the belt like a snake across her back, twisting down to her hips, drawing across the curve of her ass and trailing off to the bed, mid-thigh or so. She moaned and squirmed within the confines of her ropes. I smiled and cursed us both again.

"Time," I said barely above a whisper.

"Thank you, Jack," she replied in kind.

I hit her.

Soft and gentle strikes across her ass to warm the heart and soul. Pink ass ripe after a dozen lashes and my belt felt good in my hand.

"Thank you, Jack," she said again, low voice present and drifting.

"Time," I replied.

One quick draw, one swift arc and a deep red stripe formed across her ass.

She held her tongue and I watched the vibration sift through her body.

"You're a good bitch, Mom," I said with truth.

"Thank you, Jack," she replied with love.

I paused for effect and reflection.

"Time," I thought, knowing I'd said the word.

An identical strike deepened the line across her ass, dividing her in two. She cried out once and took three breaths to calm her heart.

"No more words," I said to myself as well as her, then I hit her again without warning.

I paced the arc around the bed, from side to foot to side, and listened to her cry. A moment of consideration stayed my hand and pain replaced violence in my stomach. I pushed her damp hair out of her face and kissed her cheek.

"I love you," I said, placing my hand over her nose and mouth.

For a second or two, or more, but just a taste, nonetheless. I smiled nothing at her and said the same. Her blind eyes widened in shadows, as if in that instant she saw through the blindfold and into my heart. She relaxed, to my surprise, as if I'd silently granted her the greatest freedom of all.

I released her and she gasped, coughed and cleared her throat. "I love you, too," she said, raspy and incomplete.

I smiled in return and picked up a rolled pair of athletic socks and another tie: the last items I had prepared. I knotted the socks in the middle of the tie and shoved the mess in her mouth, cranking it tight behind her head.

Violence returned and my belly felt weak, sweet and sour. I held the belt in my hand and told her I was going to hurt her again.

She nodded and didn't try to speak.

I lashed her seventeen times and wondered why I stopped.

Her red ass trembled and felt hot to the touch. A half dozen welts marked her, and in that moment I claimed her as property and knew she wouldn't disagree. Four months since Dad left us – *seventeen weeks* – a voice in my head corrected.

I didn't move an inch and found myself holding my breath in the hallway. The strange darkness consumed me. Different shadows covered the plastic windows. Different colors hid from my heart.

Just as well. I had to release her, remove her gag and blindfold. I had to hear her voice, just then, right then, so I turned and found her already free. My name, "Jack," in her voice, on her lips, rolling off her tongue. "Wonderful," she added with bindings cut, freed as if by will alone.

I looked down and found the knife in my hand, and I sensed her freedom in me.

She looked in my eyes and shrank back, fear and horror carved into her face.

I didn't ask her why or what, because I didn't give a shit one way or the other. I punched her in the mouth and knocked her back down on the bed. I fell upon her like an animal, slamming my cock into her, growling at her – *fuck* – drooling on her, spitting on her.

My cock was so fucking hard, so fucking hard. The bastard wouldn't cum. It just wouldn't cum.

I couldn't cum and I couldn't stop fucking her. Harder, stronger, bigger, faster, I couldn't stop fucking my mother. I fucked her with irony and cruelty, with wicked intent and spite. My cock swelled with white hot blood and who the fuck was I kidding?

She sobbed uncontrollably and tried to beat me off her. She begged me to stop, pleaded with me and cried inside me. Her nails dug into my flesh and her eyes burned into my heart.

I couldn't cum, so I beat her and fucked her harder. I sobbed and choked her and thought about breaking her neck. I peeled her off my cock and slammed her against the head board – then the hallway, then something else, the kitchen, something again, the family room –

In Dad's chair, panting, growling in my belly, somewhere wicked fingers wrapped around my guts. "Jackie," a voice inside my mind, searching, testing, tasting. *Kill it*, then, *kill the voice, the source, the strength.*

"*Jackie, sweetheart,*" a voice again from nowhere, no – from everywhere, no – from inside. "*It's me, baby. It's Momma.*"

"Mother's dead," I said with nothing in my heart. "An old whore now with a dried up hole."

Crying, and I knew my words were real.

Fuck.

Mom curled on the floor in front of me, all too real, collapsed and shaking, silent tears twisting her mouth.

I got up and turned on the lights. I turned on every fucking light I could find while Mom sobbed on the family room floor. I went down the basement, turned on all the lights, and came back up stairs.

Still crying, curled and fading.

I knelt beside her and she curled more. "Mom," I said, finding the word grotesque and inhumane.

"No, Jackie. No," she said, anticipating me and saving herself from insult.

Mom opened her eyes and looked at me. Her cold, swamp water gaze soaked us both to the bone. She pushed herself up and cupped my face in her hands. "Don't ever apologize to me, Jackie. I love you so much –"

"I love you, too –"

"I know you do, sweetheart. I know you do."

We slept on the family room floor with all the lights on.

In the morning, I called my dad and told him I wouldn't be coming in for a few days. His disinterested voice said he'd long since given a shit about what I did or didn't do.

I turned out the lights in the morning, fucked Mom and took a bath.

She cooked breakfast and asked if I'd hurt her again today.

"Yes," I said.

I always said yes.

Chapter 19

Wake up. Vomit. Fuck Mom. Hurt Mom. Fuck her some more. It had turned into a daily ritual. But it was the details that almost killed me. *God is in the details*, someone said.

Asshole.

"Jackie?" she asked from the bathroom. She'd been in there with the door shut for quite a while, I realized, when she called my name. I stood by the door, said nothing and waited.

"Jackie...?"

"You okay in there?" I asked, testing the door with my fingertips as if it was going to explode.

"Jackie, there's no toilet paper. There's some in the pantry on the floor. Please."

Toilet paper.

Not exploding bathrooms.

Not exploding minds.

I fulfilled her request and waited like an idiot by the door for no reason other than her appearance.

"This is so sexy, Jackie," She said as she opened the door and breezed passed me, across the hallway and into the bedroom.

"What?" I said to the smell of shit she left behind.

"God, this is so *sexy*," she said again. "Come in here."

"What?"

"Come in here."

She sat cross-legged on the bed amid cum, booze and sweat stains and asked me to sit. "Jack, I'm your mother," she said, and I wondered where she hid the drugs. She waved her hand and almost laughed. "You know what I mean. I'm your mother and we're having great sex. I mean, this is the best sex I've ever had in my life."

Before I could think, she leaned over, kissed my cheek and blurted to the world, "My own son is the best fuck I've ever had!"

Then she laughed.

And I laughed right along with her.

I laughed my fucking ass off because it *was* goddamned funny. We laughed our asses off until I backhanded her across her face. I grabbed her arm to keep her from tumbling off the bed and yanked her back into position.

"Are you kidding me?" I said to her smiling face, to her rolling ocean eyes, to the maniacal tone of her voice. I opened my mouth to say something, to say anything, but nothing came out. I did not seem to have a damned thing to say about any of it. Or I didn't know where to begin, let alone end.

And she was talking again, "You love fucking me, Jack. Admit it. You love fucking your own mother." Then she yanked herself away in feign escape. "You love hurting me, and you love fucking me –"

I slapped her and she laughed.

"I love it when you cum in me, Jack. I love it when you cum in my *cunt.*"

She laughed and I slapped her again.

"You love hurting me," she said, quieting down and rubbing the side of her face. "See? You love hurting me as much as fucking me, Jackie...."

I called her a whore after a moment or two and sat on the bed next to her.

She didn't laugh and it didn't matter.

Mom curled up next to me and rested her cheek on my shoulder. "I love you, Jack. You're my son and I love you."

She looked up at me, eyes so seriously green, and my stomach shrank. "You know that, don't you, Jackie? You know I love you with all my heart?"

I nodded and said nothing.

"Together forever," she said. "That's what we are, Jackie. Together forever."

Together Forever was the inscription on her wedding ring.

"I'm hungry," I said as I peeled her off me. My sour stomach wanted anything but food, but I had to move, I had to do something, walk, run, scream, cry. I needed something, somewhere but I had no idea what to look for, let alone what the hell was going on in my head.

"Let me fix you something," Mom said, scampering off the bed after me like a twisted pet aching to please. "I can –"

"Please, Mom," I said quietly, taking her shoulders and forcing her to look at me. "Just, *please*, okay?" I released her shoulders as if she would stay in place, as if I locked her in position. "I'm okay. I just need – I'm okay – okay, Mom? I'm alright –"

"Jackie...."

One step backward to the bedroom door and I turned and all but fled down the hallway and immediately ran out of space. I stood in the kitchen, then the dining room, then the family room, then what?

I stood in the corner by the television set – with my hand on the bookshelf my Dad had built and I wondered why there was no *fucking* door here, no hidden passage, no cave to crawl into, no cliff to jump off.

But I was already falling. Or suspended, or immersed – I hated her, I hated myself – and she was upon me like a mother, like *someone's mother*, hugging me, wrapping her arms around me, pushing me deeper into the corner with no escape – telling me how much she loved me and how perfect I was.

My twisted body churned and threatened to cover us both. I pushed her away once, then twice but I could not manage a third. She wrapped her arms around me again and for an instant realized what she'd done.

"Oh, Jackie...," she began, but where could she take it? Where could she take the name she'd given me? Where could she take the name she cried out in agony and ecstasy? Where could she take the name she snarled and spit back at me?

I hugged her back and said nothing. I couldn't tell her it was all right, that everything was all right or would ever be right again. I held on to her and expected her to save me. I expected her to save me under the sheer force of my own will.

Save me, goddamn it!

... save me....

So, I hugged her, and I cried in the corner with no escape, wrapped in Mother's arms, because I didn't know what else to do. I looked into her dirty green eyes and saw Mom staring back. She was there, hiding with me, looking for a way out of her own corner, looking for any means of escape.

"Oh, Jackie," she said again, covered in tears, as we wrapped ourselves together forever.

"It's okay, Mom," I told her, petting her head as she lay in my lap. For a moment, I thought we'd just sit and – I didn't know – just sit and it would be over, ll of it, this, whatever it was, it would just be over. I saw us both inside, or saw *it,* the end, some sort of end, inside us both.

It would be fitting to just stop, to just be in the corner with no escape but each other, to just be without words or thoughts or deeds, to simply stop.

If I just held her long enough, if I just hugged her long enough, or hard enough, or gentle enough, or in the right way, in the right position, everything would be over.

She put her hand on my cock and her mouth on me a moment later and everything rushed away, speeding, escaping, racing away – and, no. No. No!

Not now, I told her inside where she couldn't hear me. And again, *not now with the end upon us, within us, with no cliff to catch, surrender or spare us.* I rested my head back in the corner and let her draw me into eternity. I petted her hair, rubbed her temples and let my cock rage inside her mouth.

Even this, I told myself, pushing a few stray hairs off her face and watching her lips compress and release around me, wasn't real. None of this was real. None of this was real and none of it mattered.

At my insistence, nothing mattered, and I didn't know what *real* meant, and it didn't matter. Illusions, tricks, games and lies, I shifted her in my lap and slid more of me into her.

Reality wasn't an illusion, my voice, her voice, a voice said. *Reality simply did not exist.* Not this reality, anyway.

Mom pulled off and licked her lips. "You're so good to me, Jackie," she whispered, laying her head back down in my lap.

I closed my eyes and tried to cry, but clean, sweet emotional rescue would not come. So, I dug my fingers into her scalp and pumped her skull for pleasure.

Blood poured into my cock and released throbbing pain throughout my body. She moaned in obvious satisfaction. I closed my eyes and imagined my cock literally exploding in her mouth: blood, cum and ripped flesh choking her, filling her stomach – or just exploding and taking her head with it.

Exploding and taking both our heads with it....

I let go of her and found a measure of disconnection. Images flashed inside her, monsters and children, sinners and saints all reaching, feeding, twisting and turning, feeding on her as she fed on me, destroying her from the inside no matter how much of me she devoured, no matter how much of her son she fed to the monsters inside.

I *heard* the crying inside her, the screaming, the mania. I *heard* the monsters enraged, the animals in attack. I heard it and felt in my bones – and, fuck, if I didn't feel it in my guts, in my heart, in my goddamned soul.

War, I thought, groaning once at the intensity of her current task. I thrust hard several times to satisfy her. She settled into a rough and distorted method of satisfaction.

A war for both of us, I thought – but not against each other, and not for each other, either, but... war.

Where was my little war, I wondered, afraid, then, to dig too deep. Where was my crying demon hiding? I abruptly yanked Mom off me and cast her aside. "Make us something to eat," I said, barely able to look at her.

Mom scrambled to her feet, wiping her mouth and almost tripping over herself. "Yes, Jackie," she said quickly. "I love you." She glanced at me and looked away.

"Whore," I said without emphasis.

She ran crying from the room.

I resisted the urge to beat her senseless and sat down in Dad's old chair. Sunlight trickled in from the family room draperies and I thought of duct tape and black plastic bags.

Time.

I hated time. Minutes, hours, days, all of it measuring nothing. I found myself *standing* in the center of the family room and suddenly hating her.

I hated her and my cock was so hard it hurt. I looked at her across the dining room and into the kitchen. *Stupid whore sucking my* cock and cooking my food, buying me cars and clothes, doing anything I told her to do.

Sick, sweet revelation filled my stomach.

Stupid fucking whore.

I walked up to her while she cooked. She took a slight step back. *Okay, maybe not stupid.* She was one diabolical bitch, though, I told myself, reminded myself and determined not to forget.

Diabolical?

Really?

"Scrambled eggs," I said, watching her hand with two broken fingernails do the dish injustice. I grabbed the bottle of cooking oil and coated three fingers on my right hand.

"Jack," she said nervously, losing what little control she had of the eggs.

"Careful," I said, sliding the tip of my index finger into her asshole.

Mom stood up on her toes and I pushed my finger all the way in and held her in place. She wobbled a moment and stabilized up on her toes. "Jack," she said again, adding nothing to my name.

"What to do with you now?" I whispered in her ear. "I don't know what to do with you now that I have you. Mom."

"Jack, the food's almost done," she said quietly, turning off the stove with a shaking hand. I thrust my finger into her several times, then released her.

She exhaled, then inhaled, then seemed surprised when I pushed her over the counter and shoved two fingers into her ass. I worked her rough and violent for several seconds before releasing her, stepping back, and wondering what she'd do.

Nothing, of course.

Crazy. I was going fucking crazy and time had nothing to do with it.

She made the slightest move to push herself off the counter, so I attacked her again, this time with three fingers penetrating her in a distorted blur of speed and brutality.

Cruelty, then, of course.

Cruelty, pain and humiliation.

Or, no. All pain.

All of it. Inside, outside, hers, mine, Dad's, everyone – everyone's in pain one way or another – and why the hell should this be any different? I released her and took three steps around, putting the counter between us.

Her shoulders sagged but she hesitated because she wasn't stupid.

She was never stupid.

After a few moments, she let herself stand up, prepare our plates and turn toward me. "We haven't been to the grocery store in more than a week, Jack," she said without looking at me. "We don't have much to eat."

"It's okay," I replied without really listening to her. I let her carry my plate to the dining room. She remained standing as I sat and asked what I wanted to drink.

"Anything cold," I replied, settling in and reaching for salt and pepper.

"I love you," I said after a few minutes of silence.

Mom barely touched her food.

I ate like a ravenous predator. "You're right," I continued, indicating everything in the room with my fork. "All this is sexy."

Still, nothing.

"Now, do I like hurting you as much as fucking you?" I asked with mock concern and fake consideration. "I think you're right again. The two go together like apple pie and hand grenades. I can't imagine having one without the other."

Still, nothing, although she adjusted her posture and took a few more bites of food.

"But, *together forever*, Mom, really? Isn't that the inscription you and Dad have on your wedding rings?"

She folded one hand in her lap and toyed with her fork in the other.

Pick, pick, pick, I thought. Keep picking. I pushed my empty plate aside and told her to refill my coffee. She obeyed immediately and completed the process in seconds.

"I enjoy hurting you more than fucking you," I said, as she resumed her seat. An unexpected frown creased my forehead and I wondered if I lied.

"I didn't... no, I... Jack." She stopped after my name and lowered her head.

"The pain's the thing, isn't it?" I asked, bringing up words from the pit of my stomach. "I mean for both of us. The pain's the thing."

"Jack, I –"

I leaned toward her and snatched her words away. "I love you, Mom."

"I love you, too, Jack," she replied too easily. Her heart wasn't in it. Mine wasn't either, but we weren't in this for truth – and that part went unspoken.

"Clean up," I told her, pushing myself away from the table. "And we'll test our theory."

From my father's bed I listened to her cry as she cleaned. I reached over, lit a cigarette and waited for the end.

Chapter 20

Constant darkness unraveled us both. I couldn't remember when my muscles didn't ache or my stomach didn't hurt. Mom winced at the slightest movement, and she looked every bit her fifty-seven years, plus ten – and makeup just made her look like a freak.

I slid my exhausted cock out of her and she didn't move. I sat back, pulled dirty bed sheets around me and watched her sleep. *More*, I thought. There had to be more to it than this; more to it than the maniacal shit we'd been doing to each other. *This could go on forever*, I thought, and my stomach tightened.

Together forever.

I peeled myself away from her and took a long, hot shower. The house was filthy, the bathroom exceptionally so, and the kitchen a close second. I refused to remove the black plastic from the kitchen and dining room windows. I refused to throw open the drapes and doors and let the world back inside.

"Jackie, please let's open the house and get some fresh air," she'd said a few days ago.

"No," I remembered saying.

"It's so dirty in here, sweetheart. I could clean it for you. Let me clean up, just a little."

"When I'm done fucking you," I'd said, "you can do whatever you want."

She cried.

Everything made her cry lately.

Blah, blah, blah.

I never stopped fucking her, that was the thing: eat, sleep, shit and fuck – and I didn't eat much and I hardly slept. Somewhere along the way she stopped telling me how much she loved me and how perfect I was.

I sat on the garden tractor and wondered how I got there. *Fuck it*, I thought, opening the overhead door and discovering gentle rain. Strong, deep earth filled my lungs and threw me into a coughing fit.

Fuck the grass, anyway.

I pushed the garage door button, waited for the big door to close and went back into the house. Mom was right, of course: The house smelled like a shit hole. *Something exceptional*, I thought, as I stripped off my clothes and watched her wheeze and snore. I turned on the light and pulled the sheet off her. She didn't move.

I rolled her over on her stomach. She drew one sharp breath and fell back into a deep sleep. *Something exceptional,* I thought again, *to warrant a clean house and a fresh start.*

Not a fresh start, but a new chapter. *A brand, fucking new chapter.* I snapped my leather work belt once and landed a nice clean strike across both her ass cheeks.

She squealed and scrambled – overreacting, I thought – over to the headboard.

"Come over here," I said, indicating she traverse the bed to comply. "I'm going to let you clean the house today. I'll even open the windows."

"Jackie...," she said, barely above a whisper. I didn't understand why her hands shook. I didn't understand her sense of fear.

"Come over here, Mom," I said softly. "Don't make me come and get you."

She knelt on the bed next to me. I held her head to my chest and embraced her like a faithful dog. "We'll celebrate first, okay, Mom? A fresh, new chapter in our lives – in a fresh, clean house. That sounds beautiful, doesn't it?"

"Yes," she said quietly into my chest.

I felt no struggle against time. Who could stop time but God, and he had better things to do than keeping this son's cock out of his mother's cunt. God was busy and I could take care of myself, anyway.

"Something exceptional," I said, lifting her face and giving her a long, deep kiss. I squeezed her nipple until the kiss stopped. She winced and pulled away just a second too soon. "Lay on your back," I instructed, forgetting to look her in the eye.

"Jackie, please," she said. Her voice shook as she assumed the position. "I just woke up. Can I have a cigarette? And I have to go to the bath –"

"Shut up," I said quietly, bending down and pushing her hair out of her face. I kissed her softly and smiled. "You can have a cigarette and go to the bathroom in a few minutes."

I tied her quickly to the four corners of the bed and shoved the makeshift gag back into her mouth. She started to cry and I didn't understand.

I felt as if I missed something down below, past my cock and balls, past my asshole that hurt whenever I shit. I didn't understand something and Mom cried quietly on the bed beneath me.

Her tummy pumped in quick rhythm with her soft, little cry – and a little crying wasn't so bad, I thought. A little fear was expected, anticipated even, wanted, desired.

Even desired.

I snapped my belt again and lay an even hit across the thigh closest to me.

Mom screamed through the gag and tightened her body hard against the twine restraints. Her veins bulged and pulsated. Blood flushed her skin and warmed her body into a dull red for a moment or two. Her breathing slowed to rapid gasps and she pleaded with me, through the gag, to stop.

I asked her if I was doing something wrong. I bent down to her face and inquired, "Am I not doing enough for you, already? We've barely begun and you ask for more. I don't understand."

Mom shook her head emphatically no.

I didn't know. This wasn't a game here and a game there. I wasn't *fucking with her*. I wasn't playing a goddamned game – and I felt the need to convince myself – to express to myself – of my not playing a game and losing control.

Perfect control, wasn't that the deal? I was perfect: perfect and pleasing and what? And what?

And *what*?

I hit her again with the belt, same spot across the same thigh, slightly harder.

Mom screamed in pure agony and slammed her body against the restraints.

You're perfect, Jackie, she'd said to me countless times.

But, how dare she? How dare she ascribe to me such unattainable heights, such a prescribed guarantee of failure? I denied myself the truth there was more than one path to perfection.

When she settled down into a still target, I hit her again, same as before.

She awkwardly twisted her body away from the pain and held the odd position. The twine bindings squeaked and stretched out to their limits. Nonsense babbled out from under her gag. Her eyes glazed over and a thin line of drool escaped to her clenched jaw.

I moved around the bed and caressed her other thigh. She relaxed and cried openly, clearly asking me, despite the gag, to stop.

"Balance," I said without thinking. "And breath."

She took two breaths and continued to shiver.

"If it stops raining and dries up a little outside," I said, caressing her fresh thigh, "I'll cut the grass while you clean the house."

I expected the plan to make her happy.

Mom poured her frightened, washed out green eyes into me. I felt her fear. I felt her anxious, silent cry for mercy. But I didn't know what else to do. If she really wanted me to stop, then I didn't understand any of this – and I couldn't understand it, or understand what she expected.

God, I loved her. I truly did. I couldn't imagine life without her, with her not being here, so open to each other, so open with each other: a relationship down to the blood that flowed in our veins.

How could such a relationship be replaced?

I snapped the belt and left a red stripe down her previously unattended thigh.

She managed to spit the gag out of her mouth. Words tumbled out of her in a jumbled mess of nonsense and tears. "Please stop please stop please stop! No Jackie No Jackie No Jackie!"

Something like that, anyway.

I hit her again in the same spot and forced the gag into her screaming mouth.

So loud. So fucking loud. Everything was so loud. Every church bell ever constructed rang inside my head.

I cranked the gag tighter and cut off most of her volume. I thought about blindfolding her but I needed her eyes – I held on to her eyes too tightly. *Fuck, what did she want from me anyway? How much was I supposed to give her?*

I whipped her leg a third time, then sat in the chair by the window.

Mom kicked and thrashed against her restraints, failed to eject the gag from her mouth and cursed deep and wicked profanities with her eyes.

I pushed the drapes aside enough to watch the continuing, gentle rain. I lit a cigarette and snatched the ashtray off the end table and sat back. Filtered, cinnamon light threatened the room and highlighted Mom's weakening struggle on the bed.

Fear.

I knew fear and little else, really – though I was not loath to admit it. I just had no one to admit it to that could affect my immediate distress. I smoked and ignored Mom, but then she quieted, too, in my sudden, unnerving calm – and we each found no satisfaction.

The soft sunset slowed my breathing and softened hell's church bells inside my mind. I awaited revelation and found Mom's face softly staring at me. No more tears, no more shaking, arguing, resisting. No more fear and I didn't ask her because I knew she wouldn't be able to answer.

I stood over her without having moved, without having stood up from the chair. Yet, I stood now and I slid my belt around her neck and slipped the end through the buckle. She refused to move and kept her face sharply to the side. I laid the tail down her midsection and I knelt between her thighs.

Mom craned her neck further away and drew one sharp breath as I mounted her swiftly, without appreciation, then held still. She drew another sharp breath and maintained herself well.

I curled the belt in my fist and forced her face to mine. "I feel inside you," I said, without naming her. I thrust once, then held still. "Do you feel me inside you?" I asked, immediately thrusting once and removing her opportunity to speak. "Of course you do."

I left the belt in place and dismounted without interest or concern. "I hear you crying inside, Mother – or, I see it," I said too quickly. "Either way, I see tears in your eyes, Mom. The same tears in your heart."

She said nothing and looked away.

I resumed my seat by the window and said, "Damn rain," as if I gave a shit.

She mumbled something through the gag and I ignored her for a moment or two. I mounted her again, slowly this time, and gradually tightened my belt around her neck. Worried now, I thought and smiled, and I didn't blame her.

I didn't *really* want to hurt her. Not real pain. Not authentic pain. She knew this, of course. Of course, she knew I didn't want to hurt her *for real*. I tightened the belt and watched the skin on her neck stretch.

Quick breaths and saliva escaped around the gag, but no words. She didn't try to say anything. Just fear again, understood between us.

Of course.

"Don't be afraid, Mom," I said. "I won't hurt you for real. I love you."

But was any of it true? Were there such things as a genuine absence of fear, a painless existence – and something as ubiquitous as true love?

I climbed on top of her and clumsily entered her. I fucked her as hard as I could for a few seconds, then climbed down and stood by the window. "I can't cum," I said to the world. "I just can't and I don't know what's wrong."

Something was wrong, though. I looked over at her and found her staring glassy eyed back at me. *Mother*, I thought. *Say something. Make everything better. Make everything go away.*

But she remained gagged and speechless.

"You fucking whore," I said, only knowing by her wide eyed expression I'd said the words aloud. I threw open the drapes fully then and exchanged artificial darkness for a genuine overcast evening.

Something exceptional.

Together forever.

I rummaged around on the dresser until I found the steak knife. I showed it to her and smiled, which I thought funny – and quickly cut her binds. I showed her the knife again and offered a mock frown.

"Don't move," I said with heart.

And she didn't.

"Now, quiet, when I remove the gag."

And she was.

I helped her into a sitting position and let her catch her breath. I flipped switches, and the bedroom, hallway and bathroom lights blinded us for a few seconds.

"Jackie, what are you doing, sweetheart?" she asked as I walked back into the bedroom.

"Something exceptional," I replied, and could hardly wait to find out myself.

"Jackie, sweetheart," she began with her own sense of caution. "We've had enough *exceptional* for one night, haven't we?"

Food, I thought. "Whore," I said.

But this time she didn't cry.

She kept talking. "I'm kind of tired, sweetheart. I could make us something good to eat and we could watch television or –"

"No," I said, sitting on the bed next to her. "We have to do this, Mother." I thought twice, shrugged and left it alone.

"Do what, sweetheart?"

I took her hand and stood up. I led her into the bathroom and told her to kneel by the commode.

"Jackie...," she said and started to cry.

I let her brace her arms on the toilet seat. "It's dirty, Jackie," she said, holding on to me as she got down on her knees. "Please...."

"You are a filthy pig," I said without effort.

"Please," she asked again.

"I didn't have anything to do with it," I said, hearing myself with a different ear.

"I know, Jackie," she mumbled, openly crying now. "Jackie, I'm so sorry...."

Mom knelt in front of the toilet bowl and cried her heart out. I fetched her hair brush and hand lotion from the counter and counted the number of steps back to her: four.

"You can take a shower in a few minutes," I told her, caressing her head and dragging the brush through her dirty, matted hair.

But words had left her, or she was too overwhelmed to speak.

Either way, I set the brush and lotion down by her feet. I lifted her ass up and pushed her face down inside the toilet bowl.

"Please don't do this, Jackie," she said quietly.

"Shh, Mother," I said, caressing the top of her ass and the small of her back. I applied a liberal amount of hand lotion to the brush handle, then dug the fingers of my left hand into the back of her head by her neck.

"I love you," I said, or thought I said, and slowly slid the brush handle into her asshole.

Mom did little more than shiver as she accepted my offering in silence. Her muscles tensed and released in little bunches across her entire body. I watched her back ripple and flex as tension and fear coursed through her body like venom.

I thrust the brush hard and violent to set the mood, and shoved her face in the toilet water. Her head submerged, brush stuck proud out of her ass, I flushed the toilet and watched her hair swirl to nowhere.

Mom jerked and struggled in my grasp. I fucked her harder with the brush and kept her face submerged.

Bubbles, then, and I hadn't thought about bubbles. I hadn't thought about killing her again, either, until that moment.

I pulled her out of the toilet and left the brush handle shoved up her ass. My fist woven through her hair kept her in place, and we both took deep breaths at the same time.

Together forever.

I flushed the toilet again, shoved her face down deep and reamed her asshole until I saw blood.

Blood and bubbles.

I pulled her up, let her breathe and yanked the hair brush out of her ass. She slumped in my grip and said nothing.

So, I said, "You're not saying anything, Mom," and suspended her head over the toilet by a fistful of hair. I added, "I love you," as an afterthought, then suddenly felt overwhelmed by loss and loneliness.

She offered nothing but dead weight and fear. I mounted her from behind and drove her ass hard, alternating between flushing and dunking and slapping the back of her head.

"I love you," I said again, but I gave her no opportunity to reply.

Then, I laughed.

I laughed so hard I had to stop fucking her. I dismounted and kept her head suspended over the commode – and... I didn't know.

I didn't know... anything – something.

I didn't know something and I hit her, or was hitting her, and I couldn't stop – no, I didn't want to stop. I punched her face – slapped her, and spit on her. I kicked her, spit on her, or punched her again – both, or all three. I kicked her thigh and her ass. I kicked her in the face, then she turned, or was turned, or I turned her, I didn't know.

And I was fucking her asshole again, or cunt, or both, again, shoving her face in the toilet and telling her what a *Godawfuluselesspieceofshit* she was – over and over, and I didn't know something, or anything.

I yanked her away from the toilet and threw her against the tiled wall. She hit her head hard and for a moment I worried.

She looked up and smiled.

She smiled.

I beat her face until blood ran from her nose and mouth. I punched her until her eyes went black and swelled shut. I threw her on the floor between the toilet and the counter and raped her cunt and ass until she stopped screaming –

Until I violently threw up what little alcohol and junk food remained in my stomach. I left her on the floor, stood and staggered to the sink and vomited again.

"I can't cum," I said, and spit the last bits into the sink. I glanced at myself in the mirror and quickly looked away. "I can't fucking cum," I said, turning to face her, "and I don't know why the fuck not –"

Then, I saw her in a pile on the floor.

I remember blood.

Then, nothing.

Chapter 21

I woke up hard and fast, as if someone jolted me with electricity, and found her wrapped around the toilet in a pool of her own blood.

"Shit," I said, crawling over to her and pushing her wet, sticky hair around.

"Fuck," I said when I found her face. "Mom?" I pleaded with the universe, quickly adding an apology to God.

Fuck God, actually, I thought, and said, "Mom," again.

She moaned, groaned, opened her eyes and closed them. "Oh, Jackie...," she said in a voice dry and caked with pain. I gently unfolded her from the toilet and straightened her out. She breathed a sigh of relief and mumbled something about pain, pleasure and consequences.

I had beaten her to a pulp and fucked her when she clearly said, "No."

I had raped her.

Instant hard on.

I raped my own mother.

Painfully hard.

I didn't understand, but I fucked her then – raped her with concern – with something. *Something* on top of her while she cried and covered her battered face with shaking hands. I pushed us into the center of the bathroom floor and fucked her harder.

Again, I couldn't cum. I couldn't cum, and my cock was so hard and painful I wanted to rip it off and throw it away.

So I stopped fucking her.

I stopped fucking her, stood up and walked into the bedroom. Mom wouldn't – or couldn't – stop crying. I paced the hallway like an animal, from the kitchen, past the bathroom, into my old bedroom and back again.

Still, the same position, the same tears.

I repeated myself, but ended this time in the family room and Dad's chair.

Still, the same position, the same tears.

I crossed my legs and bounced, or vibrated, or whatever the hell it's called, in nervous unison with my rapid-fire heartbeat.

What the hell was going on?

What the hell was I doing?

I sat naked in Dad's chair and honestly considered chopping off my insane cock. I got up and went to the edge of the kitchen and looked at the knife block on the counter. I went into the bathroom and found Mom unmoved and crying at the same mournful level.

I pissed on her, or I was pissing on her, and I didn't understand any of it, and I knew I didn't have the balls to cut off my cock, and I laughed. I pissed on her face and I laughed at myself, at her, at Dad, at everyone, everything and nothing.

She didn't move, she didn't scream, she didn't yell, she didn't do a damned thing except stop crying and lay there.

"Clean yourself up," my voice said as I shook the last drops of piss onto her face.

"Jackie," she said, and I heard my name.

"Jackie," she said again, and I heard my name twice.

"Jackie," she said a third time, and I dropped to my knees beside her.

I didn't know what to do, so I took her hand and did nothing. I didn't know what to say, so I held her hand and said nothing. I didn't know what to feel, so I squeezed her hand and cried.

She squeezed my hand back and tried to roll toward me, but pain twisted her features and stopped her. I scooped her head and shoulders into my lap. We cried and said nothing, not knowing what else to do.

When the crying stopped we still said nothing, and I knew we were both thankful for the silence.

After a time, I felt her squirm and I wondered how long we slept on the bathroom floor. I remembered time didn't matter anymore, and I used the bathroom rug as a makeshift pillow when I slid my lap out from beneath her.

"A shower," I said amidst a string of unconnected words and garbage thoughts.

She understood and said, "Yes."

Slowly, we stood, showered and said nothing. Water hurt her body. The pressure of the shower hurt her bruises, abrasions and cuts. She turned and leaned into me while I washed us both.

I felt love. I loved her. She was my mother and I loved her – and I knew when she healed I would beat her again.

We both knew it.

She turned her swollen face into my chest and said, "I love you."

I said nothing and held her tight, careful not to hurt her.

*   *   *

I opened up the doors and windows and let her clean to her heart's content. For six days, I let her cook and clean and fuss about like someone's mother, like my mother, anyway. I fucked her a little here and a little there, shot dry lifeless orgasms into her and played house with her.

On the seventh day, I slapped her bruised face and called her a whore. She clutched her swollen cheek and took a step back. I knocked her hands aside and slapped her again. She brought her hands up again, and again I slapped them aside. I took a step forward and slapped her again. I slapped her face until she sought refuge under the kitchen counter and curled herself into the dining room corner.

I kicked her in the stomach, turned and took two steps toward the bedroom, then hesitated and turned back.

Mom wrapped herself into a ball and couldn't stop shaking. "Please, Jack...," she said without looking at me.

"Get in the bed," I said as if addressing a dog.

"Please, Jack," she said again.

"Get in the fucking bed."

"Jackie, Please –"

I lifted my hand to strike and she scrambled up and mumbled incoherent prayers to God. I let her pass and slapped the back of her head. "Get in the fucking bed," I said again.

She sobbed and ran toward the bedroom.

"You're a fucking whore," I said, following her down the hallway. "You're a pig and a piece of shit all rolled into one."

Everything inside shook and vibrated: My own nameless demon stood inside and laughed. Love-hate-love-hate spun through my mind and body, eliminating details and churning my stomach into garbage. Thoughts and feelings melted into little more than impressions, estimations and guesswork.

I found myself in the bedroom, whipping Mom with something – with my belt, I saw, buckle tight in hand, strap curled out in attack. I whipped her until she stopped defending herself.

Then I stopped and growled something I didn't understand and caught a glimpse of movement outside the window. Mom slid off the bed and sobbed at my feet. I ignored her and watched a car leave a dust cloud down the dirt road. A red car of some kind, of any kind, then nothing, and only the dust cloud remained like a long dissolving snake.

I dropped the belt and turned back to Mom. She sobbed at my feet, curled herself around me and begged me to stop. I pulled her up by her hair and threw her back on the bed. She screamed and tried to scramble away. I yanked her back by her ankles and spanked her ass several times.

"Should I pick up the belt?" I asked with someone else's voice. Somebody, something, and just too many conversations in my head. Something clawed inside my body and, after months, I felt at home.

Mom said words I didn't understand or refused to hear. She pleaded with me, begged me, for something, for nothing, for everything. I didn't understand her, as if she spoke a different language. I shrugged inside and spanked her ass until my hand went numb.

"Please, Jackie," she said, and I understood my name.

Please, Jackie, I thought, or ignored, or something, as I raped her asshole and punched the back of her head. I dug my fingers into her scalp and increased the brutality.

Monstrous, inhuman sounds poured out of her and flooded my brain, scrambling my thoughts and feelings into gibberish. She snarled like a monster and strained her neck at my pointed attack. Light, dark, morning, midnight, time swirled and flushed itself down the toilet – and I could not let her go.

I screamed incoherent nonsense back at her and dug my fingers deeper into her skull and hip. Black-white-black-white, so much black, pinpoints of light leading nowhere. I smelled blood and raped her harder. I lifted her hips and pulled her back into my violent attack. Fear, hatred, pleasure, pain screamed inside my body –

– and I was parked on the road a mile from the house, engine off, one hand calm, one hand shaking on the steering wheel. The stench of blood and violence filled the car. I leaned out the window and threw up. No dream, I told myself, no fantasy –

– her ass ran thick with blood, coating my cock in a thin, putrid layer of slime. Screaming, crying, loving, hating, emotions smashing together, simple fear and bullet holes through my soul. A gun, I thought, to rid the world of evil –

– madness, all of it. *Motherfucker me.* Rapist, whore – and fuck Dad, too – and why am I in this fucking car? *I'm not in the car*, I told myself, stretching and bending truth. *I am home raping Mom.*

Except the car engine started. I felt vibration through the steering wheel. I felt life in the seat of my pants. I shivered once and tried to shake it off – to shake everything off, shake something off. I didn't know – I didn't know what to do.

I didn't know what the hell to do.

So I drove the Trans Am.

Gravel road fishtails, blown stop signs and strained suspension – bright tan dust filled my rear view mirror. Fourth gear came too fast and I fought the car from going sideways into the ditch. I drove a two mile block of farms, cattle pastures and broken barns and ended up back where I started, except facing home.

One quick thought of Mom stiffened my cock. Nothing, in fact, *could* get my cock hard *except* her. If I killed her I'd never have to worry about a hard on again. Or, if I killed myself, for that matter. Or both of us.

I drove the Trans Am up the driveway and backed it in next to my old car – my *actual* car, not some fucking, fairy make-believe bullshit car. I walked into the garage and stood there. Then I sat on the garden tractor. Then I sat on my old motorcycle and played with the clutch and gears.

Fuck, I didn't know what to do.

Rape and murder and a cock rock hard in my pants led nowhere, at least in combination. I rocked the motorcycle back and forth and considered the door into the house. *White*, I thought. The door was very white.

Had it always been like that? So bright and white? I never painted it. Dad, then?

The door was so goddamned white I wanted to rip it off the hinges and – what? I took a breath and – what? I set the motorcycle back on its kickstand and confronted the door directly.

You bastard door, I projected. *Protect us who cross your threshold, comfort us who dwell inside.* I felt like an idiot for a moment or two, then I slowly twisted the knob and let the white door swallow me whole.

She was there, of course, Mother dear, barefoot and almost naked, waiting as if she'd known the moment I'd return. She didn't turn and run. She didn't scream and cry. She didn't fall into my arms or drop to her knees and suck my cock. She stood perfectly still, smiled and said, "I knew you would never leave me."

Her words penetrated like a curse. Invisible weight sat on me, and I knew she was right. I wouldn't leave her. But there was more to it than that – more to it than protection from loneliness and demon sex.

She was crazy and I had gone crazy with her.

"I love you, Jack," she said, taking one tentative, frightened step toward me. "I'm your mother and I love you."

I closed the distance in one step and slapped her face without enthusiasm.

"I love you," she said again.

I slapped her again and called her a bitch.

"I love you."

I slapped her again and called her a whore.

"I love you."

I slapped her again and called her a slut.

Tears filled her swollen eyes and she wrapped her arms around me before I could react. "I love you," she said again into my chest.

I struggled to untangle myself from her. I called her a cunt and couldn't break free without hurting her. "You fucking cunt," I said again, but the words came out flat and useless.

"I love you, Jack," she whispered in my ear.

"I love you, too," I heard myself say, and we cried in each others arms.

I beat her and fucked her through the night, and in the morning I went to work because I didn't know what else to do.

Chapter 22

I went to work and came home.

I was home now, sitting in the car.

I knew I went to work.

I *knew* it.

I knew it because the dash clock read four-thirty. I remembered leaving for work at seven – *seven oh-four.*

I saw Dad. When I got to work, I saw Dad and we argued like usual. Within minutes, we exploded all over each other. Fifteen minutes later, I was on my way home. An hour there, an argument, an hour home – except it was four-thirty.

Nervous energy slithered down my spine. I switched on the ignition for no apparent reason and AM radio news blasted – *blasted,* out of the speakers. I didn't remember listening to AM radio news. I fumbled with the radio knob and told myself everything was fine.

My gas gauge came to life with the ignition and read almost empty. I had a full tank when I left for work –

Enough.

Please.

I grabbed the keys out of the ignition, climbed out of the Trans Am and headed for the house.

Food. I needed food.

I needed something, I thought, watching my hand shake as I reached for the door into the garage. Summer sun and a silver-blue sky drew my eyes overhead and I caught a glimpse of a hawk circling far overhead – circling something, gliding, hunting, searching for the kill.

I absently twisted the door knob and almost fell into the garage.

Mom's voice hit me from every direction. "Jackie, where've you been? Your father's coming home tomorrow and we have a million things to do."

Her words hit me rapid fire and I staggered back from the ambush. What the hell was she doing in the garage anyway? Taking out the garbage? And what the hell was she saying about Dad?

"You mean he's coming for a visit tomorrow?" I asked, shutting the door with slow dedication. My hand wouldn't stop shaking – *That hand,* I thought, *the right one.*

"He's moving back," Mom replied absently. She took a breath and averted her eyes. "He's moving back, Jackie. Isn't that wonderful?"

Then she looked up, but only for an instant – enough for a genuine smile, then she dropped the garbage into the can.

"Moving back?" I asked slowly, noting her white Capri pants and tennis shoes.

"I've got your clothes back in your room," she answered with a simple nod. "But you have to hang them up, and you've still got things in the dresser – and I need help turning the mattress –"

"Mom –"

"We just got off the phone a little while ago, your father and I. Whatever you said to him, Jackie –"

"Whatever I said?"

"Yes," she answered quickly. Empty energy poured out of her, as if she'd drawn herself into a vacuum. "Won't it be wonderful to have him back home?"

"I –"

"Now, go on, put the rest of your clothes away."

Mom dropped the lid on the garbage can, turned and faced me. She took an obvious breath and looked me straight in the eye. "Don't just stand there, silly. Now, go. Shoo."

She shushed me toward the door like the family pet.

Or her son.

I didn't move, or couldn't, and bore my gaze back into hers. "What the hell's going on, Mom?"

"I told you. Dad's coming home –"

"No, Mom," I said, taking one step toward her. "What the hell is going on?"

"Jackie," she answered, shushing me again with the tone of her voice. "Don't be silly, dear –"

I reached her in three more steps, dug my fingernails into her shoulders and shook her once. Our eyes locked only an instant. A blue-green ocean buried all the life inside her.

"Jackie, you're hurting me," she said, turning her face away. "Please, Jack. Please let me go."

Please let me go.

I held her still, held us both still, a moment longer. I caught her again by the eyes and found a stranger staring back. Something, someone, inside me, deep inside my own reflection I found someone else, someone I didn't know. I released her and entered the house before either of us could respond.

Then, lights, all of them, at four-thirty in the afternoon.

Every light in the house was on and brought back shadows I hadn't seen in months. *None of this shit matters.* I resurrected a monster for every shadow and imbued the lot with the power of my destruction. Except nothing attacked. Not a scratch.

None of this shit matters.

I bowed inside to my shadowed audience and found myself in my bedroom. *Six years in this house, and this is my bedroom.* My bedroom of six years, but what did it matter? *Six years, six months, six days, six hours, what did it matter?*

"Jackie," Mom said from behind and I nearly turned and slapped her. Reflex more than anything, I told myself, but I was sorry I hadn't done it. I ignored her and laughed at the pile of clothes on the bed.

I laughed at the bed itself, at the dresser and the desk. I laughed openly at the entire fucking room because none of this shit mattered. None of it mattered. How could any of this shit matter – this kind of worthless shit –

"Jackie?" She turned my name into a question because she wasn't completely dead inside.

I turned sharply and stared into her invisible eyes. "Mother?"

She relented and pulled back – or was it something else I saw in her eyes? The surface of the ocean reveals nothing of its depth. Weakness, then? Hers or mine? Both, I thought, or guessed, and immediately I didn't care.

When knowledge speaks, wisdom listens. I said nothing, heard nothing, felt *almost* nothing. I slapped her face once and she fled the room in tears. I didn't understand – any of it.

She returned and screamed, cried and screamed again. Her words slurred together and I stood motionless without understanding. She left the room crying, again.

The blink of an eye, a turbulent green eye, and I laughed again. I laughed at the clothes on the bed and couldn't remember the last time I smoked a joint.

Then I went after her.

Mom looked horrified, wide-eyed, terrified, every bit the b-movie victim. She crumpled into the corner by the door to the garage and sobbed without direction.

I didn't lay a hand on her and didn't say a word. I looked at her broken white heels, the ones she broke in the car, then back to her.

"Jackie, I'm so sorry I got cancer," she said.

Cancer? What?

"What?"

Then, "What?"

"What the hell with the shoes?" I said, asked and dismissed. I kicked the shoes too late for impact. The cancer was four years ago. I forgot words as soon as I said them, or maybe I didn't say them at all.

Then, *God,* I thought.

God.

I could beat her and rape her and beat her again and none of this shit mattered, anyway.

"Jack."

What?

"I didn't want it to stop, Jackie, but the cancer...."

Like a sentence missing words, or something – out of step, tempo, rhythm, something – again with the *something.* Always with the *something.*

She looked away as if she'd exhausted her message.

I shrugged and found no words for either of us.

"We have so much to do, Jackie," she said and I couldn't disagree.

I left her by the door and decided on breakfast for dinner.

Epilogue

She crossed her legs just so because she knew I wanted to fuck her – or would fuck her – like a duty or some shit, an opportunity, reward, punishment, whatever. Actually, I told myself all that shit to avoid screaming like a maniac and ripping my own head off.

So, "I would fuck you," was the first thing I expressed after we met in her office.

The awkwardness of it all surprised me. I used words like *capable* and *visual* and immediately revealed a certain separation inside. My beautiful, sick, twisted fantasies spiraled into distorted memories, lies, half-truths and destruction.

Memories of Mom returned to me like a washed up, forgotten piece of paper discovered after the laundry: A fuzzy, obscure message with the information gone or distorted and the experience hazy and incomplete. I held only an image of the truth in my hand, like that paper, or in my head, really, and I ran it back through the washer in my mind until it dissolved down the drain. But the fuzzy, obscure part remained, and some of it, much to my despair, cleaned up quite nicely.

"Write it down," my would-fuck therapist told me. "The best therapy comes from your own words." So, I wrote the pornography of my life and emailed it to her. During my visits, we never talked about anything specific that I wrote, and I wasn't entirely sure she'd even read my words, but the process opened an old, forgotten wound and bled my life out all over the page.

A year later, I sat on her couch and defended divorce with my wife sitting next to me. Words went on in between, I'm sure, but nothing exceptional comes to mind.

"You're giving up," one of them said.

"You're not giving yourself a chance," said the other.

I wrote a lot of stuff down during that year. I threw a lot of stuff away and burned up a lot of words and energy. But, in the end, on the couch, nothing.

"You don't understand," I said and left it flat between us. *Pointing at the moon,* I thought. All I could do was point at the moon and scream inside, *My finger is not the moon!*

"She's not your mother," said the first.

"I'm not your mother," said the second.

Closure, of course. Everyone needs an ending.

"She loves you," said the first.

"I love you," said the second.

I said nothing and lost myself in a deep green ocean.

Jane

Sunday night panic, but only at first, in the beginning, when Janey thought something would be done, when she thought her mother would save her. Later, only submission, confusion and the acceptance of flexible truth sustained her.

"Monsters are real, Mama," the girl insisted, tugging on her mother's apron because her life depended on it. "Monsters are real."

Crying now, from deep inside her belly, when Mama ignored her and continued to wash the dishes, when she realized nothing would be done to save her. "Please don't make me go back," she begged, tugging harder on the apron. "I'll be good. I won't eat much food, Mama. I promise –"

Stop.

Mama stopped the whole thing with the glare of her dirty green eyes. The stout woman bore down on her youngest daughter without pause. "What are you talking about, child? You're going back. Make no mistake. We're lucky to have the Sisters in times like these." She turned back to the dishes and looked out the dirty window. "God bless President Hoover," she said to the air, the sky, to whatever she found outside the window.

"But, Mama," Janey persisted, half crying and shaking. The nuns were so nice, she agreed, and she loved each and every one of them, except maybe Sister Marble, who, aside from having a funny name, paddled her into tears for stealing a cookie. "But, Mama...."

Mama sighed and dropped the dishrag in the sink. She turned to Janey and pushed her eyes right through her daughter. "But, nothing, child. We're all suffering. We're lucky to have Father Szymanski and the Church."

Janey sobbed at the mention of the Father's name. "He's the one," she tried to say, but she spit out only tears and jumbled words. *He was the monster,* but she couldn't get the words out.

Mama grabbed her shoulders and shook her. "What are you saying, child? Are you causing trouble at the orphanage?"

"No, Mama –"

"You better be a good girl," Mama said without giving her time to answer. Her green eyes flared and burst into flames, and Janey felt her mother's presence flood into her body. "Father Szymanski is a Saint –"

"No, Mama!" the girl blurted through tears. "He touches me. He makes my belly hurt –"

One hard slap silenced Janey. Mama let go of her daughter and straightened her back. "Watch your mouth, child. That man's a saint." Mama glared down at Janey as if waiting for a reason to hit her again.

"But, Mama –"

Mama slapped her again. She grabbed her daughter's arm and hustled her out of the kitchen. "I don't know where you get your ideas, child," she said, taking the thought nowhere. Her fingernails dug deep into Janey's arm, and the girl squirmed and tried to keep up with her.

But it hurt. Everything hurt so much.

Family pictures lined the old, washed out walls of the hallway. And every pair of eyes looked right through Janey and into her heart. She didn't mean to be a bad girl. She didn't understand why Mama wouldn't listen to her. She didn't understand why Mama wouldn't let her speak.

"But, Mama...," she said without thinking and received another slap in reply.

"You don't let the devil into your heart, child," Mama told her as she dragged her into the bathroom.

"No, Mama, Please...."

"Denouncing men of God. *Good* men of God."

"No, Mama...."

"There is no room in this house for sinners."

"Please, Mama...."

"There is no room in this house for people who speak ill of the good men of God."

Janey caught one glimpse of her oldest sister Catherine, hands clasped together and watching from the end of the hallway. *She* knew. Catherine new. Catherine knew about Father Monster and she didn't say a word.

Soap filled Janey's mouth and sickened her belly. Her cheeks hurt from Mama's punishment and from the constant flow of tears and fear. She didn't know what was happening, or why, and everything hurt so much, everywhere, inside and out, and she didn't know how to be better, how to be a good girl no one wanted to hurt.

Janey threw up in the sink, and Mama stopped.

She stopped.

Janey felt Mama soften and release her. When she lifted her head out of the bathroom sink and looked down the hallway, Catherine smiled back with both pleasure and fear in her eyes. Her sister didn't have Mama's terrible eyes, not green anyway, like Janey did—Janey had her mama's green eyes, but she hoped her eyes didn't catch fire like Mama's. Catherine's eyes were like ice. Cold ice. Dirty ice. Catherine's eyes hurt even when she was being nice.

Mama softly stroked her hair and gently lifted her face up to hers. Gone was Mama's fire. *Her fiery spirit,* Mama called it. "Don't be afraid to let your spirit shine," she'd said so many times. But Janey still didn't understand, even as she let Mama wash her face with a warm washcloth, even as she told herself she understood the difference between pleasure and pain, she didn't understand why Mama caught fire the way she did.

She didn't understand why Father hurt her like he did, either. Mama said he was a good man, a man of God. Janey smiled back and didn't understand as Mama washed her face and combed her hair and reminded her she had to be a good girl at the orphanage.

"Another year, baby," Mama said with all the love in the world. "You'll be big enough you can help your sisters on Mr. O'Malley's farm."

Janey glanced down the empty hallway and found Catherine gone. A ghost, she thought: Mama's ghost. Sometimes Catherine's silence scared her more than Mama's fire.

Mama wrapped her in her arms, and Janey sunk into her mother's worn cotton dress. She wanted to stay there forever, stay wrapped inside her mother and wrapped inside herself. "I love you, child," Mama said, gently rocking them back and forth.

Janey heard the truth in her mother's words, which made everything all the more confusing.

"Now, go get your things. Catherine will walk you to the orphanage."

New tears arrived, softer tears, quieter tears. She pressed her face into Mama's dress, into her soft belly, and cried herself out. Janey knew if she said anything more, or restarted the conversation in any way, Mama's fire would return and the pain and fear would be double.

But Father Monster waited for her, and she didn't know what to do. Mama stroked her hair and rocked them back and forth.

Janey hugged tighter when Mama began to hum a gentle, forlorn melody. The simple tune went as far back as Janey could remember, and she calmed down despite herself. *A year,* she thought and immediately tried to forget. A year was forever.

Forever with Father Syzmanski and his monster.

Mama rocked and hummed for too short a time before peeling Janey off of her. "Go get your things, child," she said, wiping her eyes and turning away.

"Why are you crying, Mama?" asked without fully understanding her own question.

"Oh, baby," Mama said into the bathroom mirror. "It won't be long, I promise, and you won't have to go away from us anymore."

"But, Mama," Janey began, then immediately stopped. Even this, she thought, wouldn't last – Mama like this, now, with just the two of them. She knew why she had to stay at the orphanage. She was too little to help her sisters, just as Mama had said. But more than that, more than helping on the farm, Janey knew she was a bad girl. She was a bad girl, and that's why Father Monster punished her.

Sister Marble didn't paddle her for stealing *one* cookie. She got paddled for *always* stealing one cookie. Janey bet she'd stole *six* cookies since she'd been at the orphanage. And Sister Marble hadn't caught her every time. She'd gotten away with it, most of the time, anyway.

Janey had gotten away with stealing.

"Go on now, child. Get your things." Mama gently spun her around and nudged her out of the bathroom toward the stairwell door. "Catherine!" Mama called out over her head, and Janey knew she was leaving now. She was going back. Now.

"Catherine! Come take Janey back to Church!"

Noo..., Janey mouthed the word as she struggled with the doorknob leading up to the room she shared with her sisters. She looked back at Mama after she climbed the first step.

"You gonna be fine, my baby," Mama said with a smile, bending down and kissing her forehead and running her fingers through her hair. Then, she released her and turned away. "Catherine!" she called out in a voice quickly running out of patience.

Janey got her clothes together, back in the paper sack, and wished her other sisters were there. She wished for *anyone* who could protect her from Father Monster. The old door squeaked when she closed it, but the latch caught with the familiar heavy clunk. Heavy. Safe.

Janey carried the paper sack full of her small life down the stairs and found Mama and Catherine waiting for her by the front door. She would show them. She would be a big girl *and* a good girl all at the same time. She wasn't going to cry no matter what or anything.

Mama hugged her, and Janey breathed in as much of her mother as she could before having to exhale it back out. Just then, the old furnace went on with a big *whoosh,* and the house cracked and stretched as if it were coming alive around them. Her room in the orphanage was always cold, and Janey fought back tears when Mama let her go of her hand.

"I love you, Mama," Janey said, but her voice was too sad to work right.

"I love you, too, child," Mama replied, covering her eyes and turning away too quickly. "Catherine," she blurted as the door closed and the girls were halfway down the steps. "You come straight home, you hear?"

"Yes, Mama," Catherine replied politely without looking back. "I will."

She always squeezed Janey's hand too tight whenever they went anywhere, but now Catherine squeezed hard enough to really hurt her. Janey tried to wiggle her fingers free, but all that did was make her sister squeeze even harder.

"Listen, you little brat," Catherine said as soon as they turned the corner away from the house. "You don't know how good you have it. We can't afford enough food as it is, without you whining and crying about Father Syzmanski and trying to come home. Like Mama says: When you can work, then you can come home –"

"I can work!" Janey blurted. "I make my own bed, and I put all the plates down *every day* at church –"

"That's not work, you idiot," Catherine said. She almost tugged Janey's arm out of the socket. "And Father isn't a monster, either. Don't you go telling Mama no such thing anymore. You hear me?"

"But, Catherine," Janey mumbled with her chin tucked down on her chest and her eyes on the sidewalk in front of her. "You said you knew all about –"

"You don't worry about what I said or didn't say. You're a stupid, little girl, Janey, and you should be thankful for Father's punishments –"

"It hurts!" Janey blurted too late to stop herself. Catherine tugged her arm harder this time, and she yelped in pain.

"Of course it hurts," Catherine snapped. "It always hurts bad girls."

"Did it hurt you, Catherine?" Janey asked slowly. "Did it hurt when –"

"Of course it doesn't hurt me – didn't hurt me." Catherine shook her head and quickened her pace, all but dragging her little sister behind her. This was such a stupid conversation, she told herself. Everything was stupid. And everybody was stupid. "Just do as you're told, Janey," she said, feeling the autumn chill shiver her bones. Her voice softened, and she hated herself for it. "If you don't fight it won't hurt so much."

Catherine hated herself when she softened, even a little. No one could hurt her, she told herself, when she was strong. Her own determination would keep her safe, and she was not going to let Janey, or anyone else, take that away.

Her sister would be fine, Catherine told herself. Her sister would be fine because she herself was fine now. *What's past is past,* just like Mama always said. Only a few more steps and she could rid herself of the ungrateful little brat.

Janey took the last few steps up to the orphanage door by herself and the waiting Sister. Janey didn't know her, but she was young and pretty. And scared, she thought. The newest Sisters always looked scared.

Janey turned to say good bye, but Catherine was already half way down the street and walking away faster with every step. "Bye, Catherine," she whispered to her sister's back. "Bye, Mama," she said to her heart inside as she turned and faced the orphanage doors, the scared new Sister and the monster inside.

About the Author

S.L. Kowalski, born in Detroit on April 1, 1962, grew up in the heating and cooling business. He worked with his father from the time he was 12 years old until he landed in a creative writing class at age 29.

Twenty-one years later, collections of words strewn about like the remnants of a madman's rampage, he discovered a small sample of his life complete in its unadulterated glory. From these words, from the story you have just read, comes the self-revelation and honesty few people share with themselves, let alone with the world around them.

He lives in love with a witch and her cat wherever they might roam, and he tries not to hold on to outcomes – or forget to feed the cat.

www.ingramcontent.com/pod-product-compliance
Lightning Source LLC
Chambersburg PA
CBHW070925130626
46555CB00001B/284